Cor
I D

Come On, Inner Peace
I Don't Have All Day!

Sachin Garg

GRAPEVINE INDIA

Grapevine India Publishers Pvt. Ltd.
Plot No.4, First Floor
Pandav Nagar
Opposite Shadipur Metro Station
Patel Nagar
New Delhi - 110008
India

grapevineindiapublishers@gmail.com
contact@grapevineindia.in

Grapevine India Publishers

Copyright © Sachin Garg, 2013

Typeset and layout design: Arpit Printographers

To Swamiji
(who made me write this book)

There is a pleasure in the pathless woods;
There is a rapture in the lonely shore;
There is society, where one intrudes;
By the deep sea, and music in its roar;
I love not man less, but Nature more . . .

— Lord Byron

Acknowledgement

It's been a privilege to have been a part of the Grapevine India story. Whenever people ask me, how have we been able to do things, I always tell them, we've been blessed with great mentors.

I'd like to start by thanking Mr Anurag Batra and Mr Nitin Aggarwal, my mentors who've guided us through this journey of bringing together books which are bringing to at least some people's lives.

And then, I'd like to thank Ms Aanchal Arora, a writer's dream as an editor, who's responsible for most things good about the book.

I'd like to thank Durjoy Datta and Nikita Singh, two talent power houses which have taken care of my peer learning department.

And my tremendous baniya family, for letting me do my own wacky thing, like that was the most natural thing to do.

Prologue

I believe that the city of Rishikesh holds more adventure than it is given credit for. It was in late 2011, when I had finally quit my job to become a full time author and entrepreneur that my love for Rishikesh truly grew. With more control over my time after quitting the job, I realized it was becoming increasingly difficult to not take the bus to Rishikesh at every chance that I got. Yes, I fell in love with the city.

I bumped into freakish backpackers, made random friends and heard some unusual stories in the time that I spent there. But more than anything, I realized that if ever there was a place tailor made for self-discovery, it would have to be Rishikesh.

The credit for the genesis of this book would have to go to someone to whom I would refer throughout as Swamiji. He has a real name and he has his own Ashram. But unlike many fame hungry Swamis and Ashram owners around, Swamiji insisted on maintaining a low profile. I understood his distaste for popularity, simply because popularity attracts the wrong kind of people and wrong kind of headaches for him. They are happy with the filtered foot fall which ensures that only genuine people show up. And they want to keep it that way.

As a result, I have changed names or have just alluded to them by their Ashram designations. I am not going to name the Ashram too. I have shared Swamiji's story in the book and people close to him might be able to recognize him; but that is done after his permission.

The idea of this book came to me on a lazy monsoon evening, as I sat in Swamiji's *kutiya*, in the middle of a philosophical conversation with him. We were discussing the kind of people who came to The Ashram. What Swamiji meant to them and what his mission in life was.

'But what brings people to The Ashram, Swamiji? When I lived in the city, I believed nobody had any time for spirituality. I come here and witness that it's almost fashionable to be broken. Young folks seem to be coming here simply because it's such a cool story they can take back to their friends.'

Swamiji always weighed his words before speaking, which was probably why every word coming from his mouth was a gem.

'There are two types of people in this world, Sachin. The first, who comprise the majority, are *simple* people who lead *simple* lives. They may or may not achieve great things through their simple ways. They wake up every morning, go about their daily chores and labour and do pretty well for themselves. If somebody were to ask them questions like *why are they here on Planet Earth*, they would frown and rush to work.'

'I know! And I have lived amongst such people all my life,' I said.

'Yes, you have. And then there is the second type. These are the people who consider themselves *broken*. They can see questions which the first type is blind to. They can have thoughts which they would want to disentangle themselves from, but they can't.'

'I can't agree more, Swamiji. But isn't it sad that this second category pushes itself into sadness and state of brokenness?' I pondered.

'The reason why they consider themselves broken could be any of the following:

1. They have had an event or a tragedy which has had a lasting impression on them. No matter how hard they try, they cannot get it out of their heads and have stopped seeing a point in all things in life. For a short while, they manage to convince themselves that they are over it and world is alright. But it's definitely not. Time coats sad memories with dust but it is bound to fly off if we don't find a permanent solution to heal ourselves.

2. They have been disowned or cheated by someone they loved. They were normal, happy people like the rest of us. But then, one act of failure or distrust or deception has left them so devastated that everything else seems juvenile and empty.

3. Forces of life, or, if you wish to call it God, has dealt a terrible hand to them and all they can do now is wait for everything to end. Someone once said that dream as if you were to live forever. But what if you know you were going to die soon? How will you sleep peacefully at night? Will you become permanently depressed or excessively cheerful for the remaining time you have?'

I listened to every word coming from Swamiji with rapt attention. Swamiji had obviously given a lot of thought to this. I was lucky to have known a man as wise as him.

'And you have taken up the mission of changing some of these lives?' I asked.

'I am too small an entity to make any significant change, Sachin. But I try to help whoever comes to me.'

'Is there any way in which I can help?' I asked him, even though I knew I was incapable of it.

'You sure can. But it would require a lot of effort and commitment from you,' Swamiji said.

'I would love to try it.'

'You are an author, Sachin. Your books reach out to the youth of the country. Even though you don't realize it, you are leaving an impression on a lot of minds. I want your next book to be based on what you have learnt staying in this Ashram. I want you to tell our story, without telling our names. I want you to help us reach out to people we have always wanted to reach.'

'I will be honoured to attempt something as meaningful as that,' I said, albeit with a withheld fear and hesitation.

'You don't seem absolutely convinced.'

'Swamiji, my concern is that even though I would love to write about what I have learnt, the people of today don't want to read about such things. I believe in what I have learnt and that has changed my life. But people are too busy watching movies and TV serials and killing time in ways they won't even realize. They wouldn't care about what is happening in an obscure Ashram in Rishikesh.'

Swamiji heard me out. And then he grew silent for a few seconds. And then he spoke, as if an idea had hit him.

'Rishi Vyas wrote The Mahabharata. Gita, which is a part of The Mahabharata is considered the biggest learning of Hindu religion. But why is it so relevant? It

14

is because when you read The Mahabharata, you know the story and the people who are talking about The Gita. You know Krishna, the person who is delivering it. You know Arjuna, the person who is receiving it. You know Arjuna's dilemma's which are being addressed in The Gita. You know the Methodology Krishna has adopted to solve them. You understand The Gita so well because it's a part of a story.'

I had a confused look on my face. I had somehow lost track of what he was saying.

'The point is, Sachin, that I want you to write a story, like you do in your books, and deliver my message through it. As Gita forms a part of the Mahabharata, I want you to weave a stimulating story, and incorporate my lessons for people. That's the only way we can reach out to them.'

And once again, I knew I was sitting in front of a genius.

* * *

15

When She Was
Not Around Anymore

It was the last day of the third year of my college. I was in the Chemistry Lab, for my final practical exam of the year, which was going to be followed by a two month vacation. I was a mediocre student and somewhere, I actually made efforts to maintain a low profile. It was my comfort zone; I wasn't fond of hogging the lime light in college. But there was one thing I didn't do averagely: I was good in the Chemistry Lab.

I wanted to become a Chemical Engineer. And we had to make crystals for this exam, something I was particularly good at.

Making crystals is not rocket science; it is a simple procedure and by the end of third year of Chemical Engineering, everybody knows the steps by heart. But to conjure the clearest, largest and prettiest crystals is an art not everyone can master. I had the hands of a magician, I was told. And half the class would be interested in how my crystals were shaping up rather than theirs.

That day was no exception. All sixty of us in the lab were raking our brains to get the finest crystals we could, with the powder of Calcium Chloride given to us. And yes, like every time, I got whopping clear blue crystals which would have found a place in a Chemistry Lab Museum, if there was to be one.

I left the lab as soon as I was done with the experiment. I didn't have any friends in the class any more.

I didn't nurse grudges against anyone in the class. My problem was the pity that shot right through everyone's eyes. Whoever I looked at, whomever I talked to, it was sickening to get hit by the reverberations of the same emotion from all four corners. Pity and friendship can never be compatible with one another.

Poor guy, the girl he was madly in love with died.

I mean, I was sufficiently shattered after what had happened. For the love of Lord, why couldn't everyone let that be *my* problem? Those constant sympathetic reminders through their humbled body language and gestures made things even worse.

But I was struggling to hold it up as sensibly as I could. I didn't spend days in bed staring at the ceiling or strolling alone on the precarious edges of my terrace. After months of starving, I was now eating properly. But the lost weight showed on me and made me look spiritless and ripped, even though the wretchedness was subsiding. I watched sitcoms on my laptop, which is a perfectly acceptable and sane pastime. Drowned in cigarette smoke, that's what guys of my age do in their rooms anyway. I didn't talk to any of my friends but I used to chat up with my Mom daily. She had come to spend some days with me when Kanika passed away. She was my biggest support throughout that traumatic phase, but, eventually, I had to force her go back to Muscat. The same reason: I couldn't stand the grief struck condolence that every move of hers glaringly offered. Just when I finished retrospecting and decided to serve myself lunch, the phone rang. It was Mom. The moment I received, two thoughts started running parallel in my head. One part of mind knew that she meant well but the other part had a huge problem with her mournful tone. She made herself perfectly eligible to be the front runner for The-Show-Samar-Pity-Campaign.

'Hi Mom,' I said, pulling myself out of my stream of consciousness.

'How are you *beta*? How is your health? How was your last exam today? I hope you have been regular with your meals.'

I could discern that she was hearing intently. I used to be a good son when she was in Muscat. Mom and I got along, we talked on the phone every now and then and I shared with her everything I could.

But things had completely gone off track a few days after Kanika's demise. It became difficult to talk to her about anything other than Kanika. The entire conversation inevitably circled around the repercussions and effects of her death on my life.

'Mom, I want to say two things to you,' I said to her. I realized it was time I took a stand.

'Hmm'

'Mom, I love you, okay? I do appreciate whatever you have done for me, and all the care you shower on me.'

'I know you respect me, *beta*. And the second thing?' she asked with concern.

'The second thing would not be very pleasant to assimilate. Mom, I know you love me, but I need some time off you. I need to figure some things out in life and I need some time to do that.'

'Hmm, I understand. But for how long?'

'I don't know yet. But I will call you whenever I the time is right. I hope you understand, Mom,' I almost cautiously implored.

'Samar, that's what a mom does. *Understand*,' she said and hung up, surprisingly without any cracks in her voice.

That's what a mom does, understand.

I knew it was difficult for her. But she would do anything to get her old son back. I felt proud and fortunate to have such a considerate mother.

My thoughts drifted back to Kanika. She was a happy memory and if I were to go back in time, I would rather have met her and lost her than having not met her at all.

But why did I have to lose her?

Such an innocent and adorable person meeting such a scary end; how do these things work?

And what egregious wrongs had Kanika done to deserve the fate she had?

Who decides who gets to live and who gets to die?

And what the fuck was I supposed to do, when she was not around anymore?

* * *

I headed back to my flat, lost in thoughts of the summer coming up. I craved to run away from Delhi for a while. I needed to pull myself out of that environment and not sit on the sofa where I had laughed endlessly with Kanika; not sleep on that bed where I had caressed her sleepy eyes, not walk on the roads where she used to teasingly brush her hands against mine while walking, not visit those places where we bonded over cappuccinos and matured over wines.

I reached my flat and messaged Saloni, asking her to come over. Being my oldest friend and a Psychology major, she understood me like no one else did. She could see beyond the-oh-you-poor-guy-who-had-lost-his-love and could talk to me about inconsequential nothings. I liked that and I needed that.

She started the conversation with cricket, and then bitched about her husband a little. She had been funny and uninhibited, right since our school days. Her marriage was, needless to say, a surprise for us. But, as Lennon says, life is what happens to you when you are busy making other plans.

'So what plans for the summer vacation?' she asked me.

We had a two month vacation starting today after the third year. Technically, we were supposed to undergo Industrial Training for these two months.

'I don't know,' I replied, almost dazed.

'Where are you supposed to be putting up for your Industrial Training?'

'I don't know. I wish I didn't have to do it in the first place,' I made a whiny face.

And then, out of nowhere, my biggest fears came true. Saloni dropped her chirpy contour and the demeanour she adopted now made a chill run down my spine: Pity, now on Saloni's face. Shit.

'What are you doing, Samar?'

'What do you mean? I am okay, okay? Don't treat me like a victim because of what happened!'

'You think you are okay, Samar. *That* is your problem Samar. When was the last time you looked in the mirror?'

I turned my head and looked into the mirror, which

was on the wall opposite me. My six foot frame looked frail after the weight shedding. My dusky complexion now looked pale. The same ruffled hair which suited me earlier now looked like that Garnier woman's hair before she uses the magical shampoo (read straightener).

'Your puffy eye bags and the unleashed beard that grows fertile as a result of pain, would scare the living hell out of any onlooker,' Saloni continued, 'Your unwashed denims don't look cool anymore and they are begging a hem around your ankles.'

I was silent. I looked into her still, no-nonsense eyes and that was the epiphany.

Realizations come to you when you are least expecting them. It can hit you while walking on the road, when you are slapped by a close friend, or when you are listening to Led Zeppelin. This realization was worse than getting an existential crisis during the act of sex, where you suddenly feel the futility of those mechanical and repetitive movements.

I had hit my low today.

And it did explain a lot of things. It explained why absolutely everyone looked at me with 'pity'. I was stunned. Saloni had spread the cards on the table, and my escapism refused to come to my rescue this time.

And I had no answers. I had hypnotized myself into believing that I was okay. And suddenly, Saloni lifted the veil. But this was the moment of realization that I desperately needed.

'What should I do Saloni? What do you think I should do?'

'Before that, we need to talk.'

'I am listening,' I said.

21

'Tell me Samar, which is the lowest point of this whole affair that you can remember?'

I thought about it. And honestly, only one moment came to my mind. I didn't know why it was the lowest because it did not induce sadness. It was plain negative and disturbing.

I was standing on the terrace of my college building, where Kanika and I had spent infinite hours, I felt an intense urge to speak to her to call her, drop an sms or at least leave a goofy wall post on her Facebook wall. The sheer impossibility of any of these settled in me. Accepting that she wouldn't ever come from behind and surprise me, living with the added guilt that I was responsible for it to some extent: Christ, it was *the* most unsettling thought ever. I stared at the crowd going about their own business nonchalantly. I would be faking my headstrongness if I say that it wasn't tempted to take a step forward and end it all there and then.

Saloni's eyes widened with unmistakable bewilderment. It was only when I looked into her eyes that I realized the intensity of what I had said. A suicidal thought is no small deal.

'Suicidal thoughts come to many of us in the heat of the moment. But the fact that you were contemplating it while you were in your senses is alarming. Your heart and mind are not at rest Samar. You need to breathe. You need to relax. You need to make peace with yourself.'

'What the hell is that supposed to mean?'

'I mean you need to attain . . . inner peace. You need to be calmer, more *shant*! That is what you need, which I don't think you can get here. You need to get out of here.'

'Hmm,' I said, introspecting.

'Can you take care of your Industrial Training if you're not in Delhi?' she asked.

'Yes, that won't be a problem. Half the batch fakes papers for the Internship.'

'Where is Roy interning?'

'Tanroxy in Manesar.'

'And how long is your internship supposed to be?'

'Two months. Starts on 1st of June and ends on 31st July.'

Saloni processed the information. Thought for a few seconds, looked up to relax her neck and then said, 'What if you extend your vacation by a month and don't come back to college?'

'The placements are scheduled in the beginning of our fourth year . . . I *have* to be back on 1st August.'

Saloni smiled just a little, and said, 'So you want to attain peace but you have to do it quickly. You are running against time too.'

'Yeah. I don't have all day,' I smiled.

'I will arrange something for you. I think I know where you need to go.'

I looked at her blankly. I had no idea that the biggest adventure of my life was about to begin.

* * *

Saloni gave me a bus ticket from Kashmere Gate ISBT. The bus was dated for the same evening. And she gave me some more papers about the place she wanted me to spend the summer in. I looked at her and she seemed very sure of what she was recommending. It was the thirty first of May.

I let her make the decision on my behalf, because I trusted her and because I felt half as efficient of taking charge of my life at that point. The plan might work out or it might fall flat. There was only one way to find out, by making the journey she was asking me to make. I didn't like the idea of sitting at home for two months anyway, so I had nothing to lose.

I reached ISBT, got greeted by the empty bus. The conductor's frown suggested that he had taken an immediate dislike of me. He checked my ticket and got busy with other passengers filing inside the bus. I cancelled the noise by plugging in music. A cute girl took the seat beside me and gave a gleaming smile. It was strange how, much to the chagrin of Kanika, I used to notice women earlier. The 'checking-out' would be as innocuous and as inevitable as it gets with humans and for obvious reasons, the girlfriends get annoyed. But now, I was surprised as to how disinterested I had become when Kanika wasn't around. I closed my eyes. There was only one person whose thoughts crossed my mind. Kanika.

* * *

I looked at her. Kanika. Her face partially hid by those bescattered tresses, she was wearing a gorgeous blue dress as we met at the South Ex that day. Her vivacious aura made her look even more irresistible.

'Listen,' I said in her ear.

'Yes?' she replied.

'I need to kiss you right now,' I said softly.

'Here, in the middle of the market?' she replied and moved her head away. 'It's India y'know? You don't want to scandalize these people, I'm sure'.

I looked at her and then my eyes fell on something. A vendor was selling walking sticks nearby. I went and bought one for a hundred bucks.

'Come,' I said to her, as I walked into a Benetton store. I was limping now, using the walking stick. Kanika looked on, thoroughly confused as to what was I doing.

I picked a pair of jeans, kept it on my shoulder and limped my way the changing room, as Kanika stood outside. I entered the changing room and exactly thirty second after entering, I concocted a crashing sound. Now I was the guy with a broken leg who had fallen in the changing room.

'Kanika, can you please come in,' I shouted from inside.

Kanika gave an apologetic look to the salesman and entered the changing room, as I opened it just enough for her to enter. And the moment she entered, my lips touched hers. And we kissed till our lips turned swollen. There might have been a couple of more crashing sounds thereafter, but it didn't matter.

I'd Be One Of Them

A full, loud laugh woke me up. The girl who was sitting beside me was now replaced by a woman. She seemed in her late thirties, had a rather fair complexion and a conspicuous nose ring. She sat there, talking on the phone and simultaneously wiping her forehead sweat.

'What are you saying?' she said in heavy Punjabi accent, in a rather obnoxious way to somebody on the phone.

I changed my track; from 'Yellow' to 'Highway to Hell' and pressed the headphones a little harder to shut her out. But she was way too loud and close.

'If I were in your place, I would have pulled his shorts down and spanked him so hard that he would have gotten piles,' she shouted into the phone and once again, laughed even louder than the last time.

I couldn't take it anymore. I pulled my earphones out and confronted her.

'Excuse me ma'am, can you please speak a little softly?'

She shrugged her shoulders, apologized offhandedly and went back to her phone. But I could sense that her volume was increasing back again and a few minutes later, she was back to her screeching high tone. I couldn't stand her annoying laughter and her incredibly loud volume. I needed to scoot my ass from there. I put the headphones in my pocket and asked her to let me go out.

'What for?' she asked me.

I was furious now. Who was she to ask me, what for!

'I am not answering that. Will you please let me go out,' I said, a little indignantly. She was wearing a white *kurta* with a long ugly blue skirt. If she were a close friend of mine, I would have pulled her leg calling it a petticoat. For a middle aged lady, she didn't fit any stereotype of her age. And I definitely didn't like her smell. I don't know what it was. Probably a cheap hair oil, coupled with her intermittent and irritating coughing.

'But where do you want to go? It's a bus, it doesn't even have a washroom,' she said.

I was fuming now.

'I need a seat change, and I need it now!' I said, firmly.

'Aww. I am sorry. I think I've been disturbing you,' the lady suddenly became softer, but not less annoying. 'Don't bother the conductor with the seat change. I will keep my phone off now, ok?'

I looked at the conductor and I wasn't very hopeful of getting another seat in this full bus anyway.

'Please let me catch some sleep,' I said to the woman.

'See, I've turned my phone off,' she put her phone in front of my face. She was seriously obnoxious.

I kept my handkerchief on my nose, to block the oil smell and tried to bring my angry heartbeat to normal.

Around half an hour later, she was talking to the guy sitting on the opposite side of her.

'This bus stops at ten in the night at Dushyant *dhaba*.

27

They have the best bread *pakoda* you can get in the whole of Uttarakhand,' she said, rather loudly.

I knew there was no point asking her to shut up and decided to suffer through the night. When the bus stopped for dinner, I made sure I sat on the farthest table from her, as she devoured those oily bread *pakode*.

As soon as I was done with dinner, I went to the conductor and slipped a hundred rupee note into his palm and traded seats with him. His uncomfortable conductor seat was definitely much more blissful than my original seat.

* * *

'We are in Rishikesh,' I heard the voice, as the conductor shook me to wake me up. 'We will stop for half an hour for breakfast here.'

I got off the bus and the same woman was sitting on a chair in front of me. I took a seat and ordered some tea and bread. I had gotten used to eating alone. In fact, I wouldn't know what to say if someone was to join me for breakfast.

We reached our destination at ten in the morning. I looked at the print out in my hand, which had the address of my destination. There was more greenery that my eyes beheld in that one look than I would find in a year in a city. People seemed rather aimless, probably because most of them were on holiday. Some kids were giggling, adding onto the happy environment. Standing there, staring at the woods over the cliffs, I expressed gratitude to Saloni in my head.

I took a rickshaw and headed to the place which was to reform my soul.

* * *

The quaint pink look of The Ashram was heavenly. The Ganges flowed right next to it. The wind ruffled my hair and at that very moment, standing there, I knew this was going to be a good summer. I had no idea what people did in this place but Saloni told me that they would give me a place to stay and food.

The Ashram that I was sent to is a not very famous one. Saloni had heard about it from her grandmother and she thought it was a good place for me. In the time that I spent there, I understood their preference to anonymity; popularity attracts the wrong kind of people and wrong kind of headaches. They are happy with what they get and want to keep it that way.

I entered the gate and looked around. There was a white small temple on my right. Right beside the temple, there was an open area, the lawns, followed by the halls of learning. This accommodation block and the small admin block flanked the academic block. On the backside of these buildings was an unimposing mess.

When I went inside the main building, the receptionist had been expecting me. He made me fill some forms and gave me an oral manual on the protocols observed in The Ashram.

'Because you are new here, you will be provided with a mentor,' the receptionist told me. 'The mentor will be someone who is well versed with the ways of this place and hence he/she will help you adjust quickly.'

I nodded in affirmation. The receptionist had the feel of a monk. He was calm and serene. He gave me my room keys, bed sheet and a blanket.

'Your mentor will come to your room in an hour.

Freshen up by then,' he said and flashed another welcome smile. I started feeling at home already.

The room, as I'd expected, had an ascetic aura to it: A simple bed, an ostensibly hard mattress, with no superfluous furniture and a small bathroom on one side. I opened the small wooden cupboard and found a yoga-mat rolled in a corner. I unpacked my stuff and went for a shower.

I let my thoughts run in the shower. It was respite to feel that constant buzz dying down a little in my head. I liked the new environment and the fresh air. And in these thoughts, I lost track of time. And only around an hour later I realized I was late to see my mentor. I wrapped my towel around myself and came out.

What I saw was the biggest shock in recent times. The annoying lady from the bus was sitting on my bed. She was now wearing a slightly ill-fitted white *salwar kameez* and was reading a book.

'Excuse me?' I said.

'Oh, hi Samar,' she said, getting up and extending an arm to shake my hand, as if she had noticed neither my half naked, half wet body, nor the fact that I had treated her badly in the bus. Although she was trying extremely hard to look neutral, that disapproving look did betray her. She said she'd wait outside. With knitted eyebrows, she was mumbling something under her breadth as she turned back to make her way towards the door; doesn't take rocket science to figure out the essence of her fudged words.

'Are *you* my mentor?' I shouted as I looked for my *kurta*.

'Seems like!' she shouted back, which was followed by her cough bout.

I wore the white *kurta* which was kept in my cupboard. I presumed it was some sort of a dress code or uniform for this place.

Once I was done, I came out and saw the lady again. She now had a calm and welcoming smile on her face.

'We started on the wrong foot. This is not how two *yogis* meet each other,' she said.

I was a little taken aback. I was so sceptical of this woman that this sweetness seemed a prank. Also, I had never been called a *yogi*. But I liked the sound of it.

'*Namaste*,' she continued, and bent her head. 'I am Vandana Manchanda. You can call me Vandana *behen* like everyone else here does. Or just Vandana, if you like. I am your mentor in this place and I want to introduce The Ashram to you today,' she said, with a composed smile which really didn't suit her. She was more of the lady who talked loudly on the phone in a bus.

'*Namaste*,' I replied. 'My name is Samar. I am from Delhi and I am here to look for inner peace.'

She seemed impressed. 'I thought you were a young guy looking for some adventure. But it seems you have an actual purpose behind coming here.'

'You can say that,' I said, and shoved it away.

'Come, let me take you around The Ashram,' she said and she gave me a guided tour. She showed me the white temple, and told me this was where the evening *arti* took place. She showed me the lecture halls and told me the sort of things we were going to be taught. She took me around the kitchen area. And then she showed me a house made of thatch.

'This is where Swamiji lives,' she said.

31

'Swamiji?'

'Yes, the Founder of this Ashram. We don't see him much now because he lives the life of an ascetic. He is renowned for his wisdom and clairvoyance. To be accepted as his disciple is the biggest achievement one can achieve in this Ashram.'

'Has anyone ever done it?' I asked.

'Some have. But even then, odds are against us.'

'What does he seek in someone to make his disciple?'

'Well, that's the peculiar part. There is no pattern in his selection of disciples. Some of them were extremely methodical and focussed, while others were notorious for their instability and waywardness. Come, let me show you the most important part of this Ashram.'

She took me to a big hall with absolutely no ornamentation on the wall but just a carpet on the floor. There was a separate rug in front which must have been for the instructor, the *guru*.

'This is where the evening meditation takes place. Let me tell you, you can sleep through your lectures, not indulge in the *arti*, and not apply stuff they teach you here, but, don't take the meditation lightly. If you get that right, it will change your life and it will change the way you look at everything. We are all trying to master it. That's the basic purpose of this Ashram. That is how this Ashram changes lives.'

I nodded, trying to agree with what she was saying. I had to try it for myself before believing it.

Thereafter, Vandana took me around to introduce me to all the other *yogis* in The Ashram. There were people from all over the world and all age groups.

The Ashram didn't require any educational qualification or nationality. They welcomed as many people as their accommodation allowed. Some people came for a few weeks, some came for a few months and others had been there for years.

Everyone had the same motive. To make peace with themselves. To achieve *shanti*.

As Vandana explained to me how my daily routine is going to be. I was only thinking that from the next morning, I'd be one of them.

*   *   *

What If Fate Doesn't Let You Choose

Our day used to begin at five in the morning. We were supposed to have a cup in our hands and stand outside our rooms. A man came and poured a small quantity of herbal tea in our cups. Yoga is supposed to be done empty stomach, so we are supposed to have only herbal tea before the morning yoga.

It takes a while to develop a taste for herbal tea, but later on, as I got used to it, I couldn't go back to normal tea. Even today, I drink only herbal tea because of the habit I developed at The Ashram.

I reached the Yoga hall at sharp six. And then, I met our instructor, *guruji*. His name was Narendra Sinha. He had been with The Ashram for twelve years now. He seemed like a simple man in his late forties, born and brought up in some small town in Uttar Pradesh. He had a thick moustache and he spoke English with a thick Uttar Pradesh accent. And in fact, he couldn't pronounce many sounds like 'sha'. For example, he would pronounce 'English' as 'Inglis'.

We carried out the Yoga asanas as *guruji* explained to us the benefit of each of those. I realized that as simple as they look, they were actually extremely tiring and taxing on the body. By eight, I was *exhausted*.

Thankfully, it was to be followed by an hour's rest. So I came back to my room, and didn't move a muscle until nine. We were supposed to report for breakfast at nine but my body would protest even the smallest movie I'd make; I decided to skip breakfast. We had lectures at ten and one more hour of rest was something I could really use.

I reached the lecture hall at ten and as I walked in, I realized everyone stopped doing what they were doing and looked at me. I wasn't sure what had happened and went and took a seat in a corner and waited for *guruji* to come.

Guruji came two minutes later, and before he spoke anything, he looked for me.

'Where were you during breakfast?' he asked me, with almost a wooden expression.

'Sir, I was in my room. I needed rest and also, I have a habit on skipping breakfast,' I said.

'Listen Samar, you are in The Ashram, and all your city-boy habits won't be accepted here. Over here, you eat when you are supposed to eat, you sleep when you supposed to sleep. You need to do everything as a *yogi* supposed to do. Is that clear?'

'Yes sir,' I said, not knowing what had hit me.

'As a punishment to this, you will have to fast today. That will make sure you have breakfast tomorrow morning.'

'Okay sir,' I said.

He then went on to talk about Yoga, but I had blanked out. I had chosen to spend a summer here. It was supposed to detox me, make me feel better, forget the negativity and become more positive. Right now, it just seemed like a very strict boarding school.

* * *

I spent the lunch time in my room again, which I didn't really mind. The ways of the hostel and my past life had made me capable of spending at least a few days without food. As I sat in my room, I wondered if this was going to work. And then, I just waited for the clock to strike two. At one, I was supposed to report at the library. And the library was full of only Yoga books. So I picked up the only book in the whole library that I had heard of, 'The Autobiography of a Yogi'.

At two thirty we had some free time, until our next lecture at four. So we chit chatted, and I tried to intermingle with the others. Out of nowhere, Vandana slapped me at the back of my shoulder. I turned around and saw a wicked grin on her face.

'Punishment on the first day itself?' she said, like she was relishing my pain.

'Not really, I could use some starving,' I said, trying to hold out that almost non-existent fat I had on my tummy.

'I love rule breakers. Before you came, I was the biggest rule breaker here. Now I think I have competition. We will make good friends.'

'What if I don't want to?' I said, with a plain face.

'What if fate doesn't let you choose?'

* * *

At four, we had what Vandana said was the most important part of The Ashram. Meditation.

I had never meditated in my whole life. In fact, I wasn't

even a big believer in the art of meditation. I used to believe it's for people who believe they are broken, while actually they're just dumb. My thoughts were about to change.

I followed *Guruji's* instructions. I sat in *Padmasana* and closed my eyes. Everybody else followed suit. I mentally pinned my attention on every body part, starting from my feet. I tightened and then relaxed every body part, releasing the captured intangible stress. *Guruji* gave us elaborate instructions, making sure that new comers could do it as properly as the veterans.

'Relax. Relax your shoulders, relax your arms, relax your chest, relax your tummy, relax your hips, relax your thighs, relax your calves, relax your feet, relax the last toe of your feet. Breathe deeply. Now, breathe out. Concentrate on your breath,' he said.

And then, I tried converging all my attention on my breath. I breathed in, and then I exhaled. And repeat. Then *Guruji* asked us to imagine ourselves in a calm, serene space. I thought about the idea, and only one place came to my mind. Goa, and the times I had spent there. My mind began to wander but I brought my thoughts back to my breathing.

I stayed in the posture for what seemed like a long time. I wanted to feel calmer and better. I stuck around to feel a higher connection. I waited with closed eyes to feel the way I was told I would feel.

But it never came. I didn't know the reason and somehow, the physical strain of that posture took a toll on my unflinching concentration. I gave up and I realized I had, in fact, been right all along: Meditation was not meant for me.

I opened my eyes and then the world almost came

crashing. A twenty one year old college student, who loved football, was now wearing a plain white *kurta* and a plain white pyjama, sitting in *Padmasana*, on the floor and surrounded by a bunch of people, mostly elders, who were making a nasal sound, which sounded like an Om.

Where was I? What was I doing here?

I looked out of the window and I could see only trees and birds chirping. It was definitely a pleasant place. I mentally pictured a map of India and imagined myself on it. But what the fuck was I doing here?

Slyly, I took my phone out of my pocket and messaged Saloni.

'Where have you sent me? This place is not for me!'

'Why? What happened? What are you doing right now?'

'I have been trying to meditate and it is just bloody not coming.'

'How long have you been trying?'

I checked the clock on the wall. It had actually been three minutes since I had started. With a smile, I decided to write that to Saloni.

'Three minutes! That too with your phone on your side? Are you kidding me?'

She had a point. Probably I wasn't trying the right way. Perhaps, I would speak to *Guruji* after the session. I knew *Guruji* wasn't really fond of me, but maybe, he would have some answers for me.

With these thoughts, I sat there with my eyes closed, with not an iota of stability in my head, waiting for the clock to strike six.

* * *

At six we had *Karma* Yoga hour. *Karma* Yoga was an hour every day that we spend in some sort of social service activity, when the whole batch did something for the society. Today's task was to clean the campus. I decided to stick close to Guruji, and hoped to get some feedback. I realized that somebody was trying to stick close to me too. It was Vandana.

When our eyes met while picking some pieces of paper together, Guruji asked me, 'How are you liking it here?' I looked at Guruji. Just this morning I had upset him by skipping a meal. And now, the calm smile on his face made me feel as if he was incapable of ever being angry.

'It's mostly nice. But I think I will take a while before I get a hang of everything.'

'What do you mean?'

'I mean, this Yoga and meditation is tricky, no? It will take me a while before I can get a proper hang of it.'

'Well, not really. I mean there is this thing about meditation. It's not about how many hours of practice have you put in. It's about how at peace you are with yourself. If you are at peace, you could reach a higher state in no time. But if you aren't, it could take you a life time and you would still not go anywhere. I would say that more than the number of hours of practice, it's about that special moment, that blink of an eye, where everything becomes clear and you get a hang of everything.'

I nodded. I didn't know if it encouraged me to perform better or made me feel more lost. In the corporate world, bosses show a carrot to an employee, which he keeps on chasing, knowing that at some point he would get the carrot. But in my case, Guruji had shown me the carrot and left me fending for it.

Will I ever get it? No idea.

'What do you think as you do *Karma* Yoga?' Guruji asked me.

I pondered over it for a few seconds and then recollected that I had been thinking about the place, and whether I fit in here or not and if it was a good idea to come here to spend the summer et cetera. As I gathered my thought to answer Guruji, he signalled me to stop.

'You don't have to answer me,' he said. 'Answer yourself. Are you at peace? Are you stable in your mind? Are you thinking about the next rag you are going to pick? Or about your past life which is bothering you to hell?'

I didn't really have to think too hard to get an answer.

Post the Karma Yoga, everybody went for a shower, to come back for dinner at eight. Hunger was beginning to become a bit disconcerting now; I could feel the pangs. I looked through my window to see if there was a way to find food outside The Ashram. There was a *tapri* a little walk away. It was tempting. He would have tea and *samosas*. But I decided against it. I decided to make it through the punishment without cheating. It would probably cleanse and detox my body, if not my mind.

So I stayed back in my room, lost in my thoughts, the same thought coming back to my mind, again and again.

Was I cut out for this place.

Still Wondering If It Was So

I had porridge and milk for breakfast the next morning, and I was too hungry to have any sort of judgment on whether the food was good or not. It was mandatory to wash your own utensils in The Ashram. It wasn't really a problem for me, as I had washed plenty of utensils in the past.

It was during lunch that it struck me, that the food there was excessively bland. I elbowed Vandana, who was sitting beside me and asked her what was wrong with the food.

'It is *Sattvik* food, Samar. It is spice-less and keeps your mind calm and composed.'

'Hmm. Okay,' I said, and looked at the *dal* which seemed straight out of a hospital canteen. This place just got even more loathsome.

* * *

I had been looking forward to the evening meditation session, possibly because on the first day, Vandana had given so much weight to it. I was beginning to believe that this was the only useful/fun/ challenging aspect of this Ashram.

I went and took the third place in the hall. Vandana

came and sat behind me like she always did. She seemed in a mischievous mood today. I knew she was definitely not going to achieve anything in today's session. But the sad part was that she didn't seem to be trying to achieve anything. A lot of people around me had accepted their state as it was. It was as if, they had reached a comfort zone and probably didn't want to reach a higher level.

I kept my phone on my right side and closed my eyes, as Guruji told me. I tried to concentrate on my breath. I breathed in and I thought about it. I exhaled and I thought about it.

I then tried to focus all my thoughts on one thing. I focused all my energy thinking about one thing.

I had no idea how long I had been doing this. The room was quiet and peaceful. The environment was laden with tranquillity as the nasal sound of 'Om' rang in my ears, calming me even further. In the middle of all this, suddenly, a sharp sound shook me up.

To my horror, it was the ring tone of my own phone. It blaringly echoed because of the pin drop silence in the room. I remembered clearly not only putting my phone on silent, but even turning the vibrator off.

I rejected the call I was getting from an unknown number and looked straight at Guruji. He frowned hard. The last thing he would want to be disturbed by would be a ringing phone of a student who joined just yesterday.

He gave me a stern look, which was equivalent to extreme anger in this place. But, within a few seconds, the wrinkles on his forehead disappeared and he went back to his meditative state.

I looked at my phone. I had no idea what just happened. I looked at the number I had got a call from. I didn't know the number. I was furious but I was clueless. So I tried to get back to meditation. But there was no way I could, with so much amazement and confusion in my head.

* * *

Today's *Karma* Yoga was gardening. Some people were supposed to pick dead leaves with their bare hands, others had to plant some plants. The remaining were supposed to add manure to the plants.

Guruji's eyes met mine, 'Samar, you will not be doing *Karma* Yoga today. Instead, you will come for a walk with me,' he said.

I was two days old in this Ashram and I had already broken two rules. This wasn't my college, and breaking rules was a rare phenomenon here. No wonder Guruji seemed very serious when he called me.

'Do you think you are able to absorb the tenets and essence of the course?'

'Yes, definitely Guruji,' I replied, trying hard to sound genuine. 'In fact, I thought I was having a much better session this evening than yesterday.'

'Then what happened. Samar? It's hard for me to understand how you can bring along your mobile to the meditation class? And not only that, you didn't even turn in on silent?'

'I know it's hard to believe sir, but trust me, I not only turned my phone on silent, but also turned the vibrator off.'

Guruji looked at me, and he seemed surprisingly convinced by my argument.

'Show me your phone,' he said.

I handed him over the phone and watched him press some buttons. And then his expression changed as if he had just realized something. We had walked some distance away from where everyone else was.

'Go and call Vandana *behen*,' he instructed me.

I followed the instruction. As I walked towards Vandana, I realized she had been expecting that I would come to her. She was digging the ground to plant some saplings when she saw me. She dropped the shovel and started coughing strongly for over a minute, cupping her face with her inside of her arm. I was so convinced that she's doing it to annoy me. I looked away and waited for her histrionics to end.

'He is calling me, isn't he?' she said, finally.

I nodded. Within a few seconds, she was walking beside me, to Guruji. The moment Guruji and her eyes met, they exchanged a knowing smile.

'You did it, didn't you?' Guruji asked her.

She smiled and nodded. She had picked my phone, turned the sound profile to 'general' from 'silent', and called me from her phone. It was Vandana's number which he had seen in my phone. Guruji understood the moment he saw the number. It wasn't my fault after all; it was Vandana's prank.

'When will you stop Vandana?'

'I never would. I don't want to.'

'I think I would have to do it this time,' Guruji said.

'No, you won't. It's not that big a crime.'

'I'm supposed to report to Swamiji everything out of the ordinary thing that happens. And this incident definitely qualifies.'

'Hmm. Right now?'

'Yes. Right now. And you would also have to come with me Samar.'

'Come where?' I asked but neither of them paid any attention to my question. They just started walking towards the lonely hut in the premises. It was Swamiji's house. Vandana and I waited outside, as Guruji went inside to have a chat with him. He came out five minutes later with the same calm smile on his face.

'What did he say?' Vandana asked him excitedly.

'From tomorrow onwards, he is going to take your evening meditation sessions himself,' Guruji said.

* * *

It was a nervous hour next afternoon at four. For the first time, Vandana seemed to be behaving herself, possibly out of nervousness. I had never seen Swamiji, but the legend was that he had withdrawn from all things worldly when he stopped seeing a point. It was rumoured that he was very intimidating. Swamiji constructed his own hut, maintained it himself, grew his own vegetables, cooked them himself and even cut his own wood for fire. I was told the only thing he took from the outside world was the saffron cloth on his body.

Vandana and I stood in front of the *kutiya*, observing how in today's world, one would deem the idea of building a house oneself as crazy.

Vandana and I stepped in. I had heard Swamiji was in his mid sixties, but he didn't seem a day over fifty. He had a shaved head, with a *choti*, hanging behind. He was sitting in *padmasana*, and was meditating. Vandana and I looked on, waiting for him to open his eyes. We didn't dare disturb him, and out of sheer paranoia, I checked

45

that my phone was on silent around a hundredth time since morning.

Swamiji opened his eyes half an hour later and he looked at both of us. He kept staring for a few seconds as if he was studying us, as if our faces were telling him about our past life, stories which only he can see. And then he lifted his right hand and motioned us to sit in front of him.

Even though he had a gentle smile on his face, there was something piercing in his gaze.

'Son,' he spoke to me first.

'*Ji* Swamiji,' I replied.

'What is eating you up? Why so much unease in your shoulders? Why have you accumulated so many negative and unwanted thoughts inside your head?'

I was taken aback. Did he say this to everyone? What made him say all these things to me?

'There is so much tension in your forehead,' he continued. 'I can see the unrest in your eyes. It's as if you are running away from something that you are here. And it's something distinct, maybe a person or an incident or a memory. It's not something vague. You know what you are running away from. And I am sure you would rather not talk about it, because you think you are a brave guy and brave guys don't talk about their inner fears with anyone. But think of me as your doctor. If you have a stomach ache, what's the point in hiding it from the doctor if you want it cured? Also, if ever there was a person who will not share your secrets with anyone, it's me,' he said, maintaining the feeble smile all throughout.

I looked at Vandana, she nodded, egging me on to spit it out. I thought about it, but I couldn't bring myself to do it. I had not talked about Kanika since the day she had passed away. I had not told my story to anyone.

'Swamiji,' I said, I came here because I needed a new environment and new faces who would not know what has happened and hence would not remind me of it. I would like to keep it that way. I request you to not to make me relive what I am trying to leave behind.'

Swamiji took a deep breath. He collected his thoughts, and only after having weighed what he was about to say, he said, 'Son, if you think you have been able to leave everything behind by coming here, I have news for you.'

I looked at him with a straight face. The conviction in his voice and the tranquillity on his face disarmed me completely. I took a moment, prepared myself, shed my inhibitions and began telling my story.

* * *

Her name was Kanika and she was a year junior to me in college. Love seemed too weak a word to describe the relationship. We were obsessed.

And then, one day, I walked into my room and I saw her with my roommate and best friend, Roy in a . . . compromising position. They were kissing. It was almost an apocalyptic moment for me. Roy was supposed to be a good guy. But from that day onwards I couldn't stand the sight of him. I regretted having not beaten him to blood then and there when I caught them.

I just took a train and ran away to Goa. Another day of seeing them around would have killed me. I partied for two days and blew all my money and didn't think of Kanika even once. And then it struck me that I didn't want to go back.

So I stayed on, in a village called Arambol, in northern Goa. I took up a menial job in a shack called Woodstock Village. I cleaned the floors, washed utensils, managed parties and what

47

not. But more importantly, I started my life afresh and made some friends I will never forget. Each one of them was from a different world. Imran was the fat cook while Joseph was the dominating, but generous boss.

I made through for a few months, until one day, as I was throwing away dirty water after scrubbing the floor, I saw her standing in front of me.

She traced me and came to live in the same resort where I was working. She tried to explain things but I would just not listen to her. She was determined.

And then, one fateful day, her asthma condition went really bad. We rushed her to the local clinic but they didn't have adequate resources to get the situation under control. It was a small village and it had its limitations. We took an Ambulance to take her to Panjim, the capital city of Goa. But she didn't make it. She breathed her last in the Ambulance.

And what really broke me was that after she passed away, I got to know that it had all been a misunderstanding. There was nothing between Roy and Kanika when I saw them. Kanika always had asthma and Roy was just giving a CPR, a mouth to mouth respiration to her in the middle of a bad asthma attack. And this is what she had been meaning to tell me all the time in Goa. I was shattered and I despised myself. I got convinced that I was responsible for what happened to Kanika. I held myself guilty of everything. People tried to convince me that it wasn't my fault. But I knew it was.

They say that cremation of a dead person is an important process because it gives the friends and family a closure. But it didn't work for me. Nothing worked for me. Kanika's cremation happened in front of my eyes, but my guilt just got more aggravated. I still spend hours every day thinking about her. I still can't get over her. I still can't revert to normalcy.

They say time is the best healer but it didn't work in my case. Months passed but people kept asking me, why the long face? Why the drop in the shoulder? Why the lack of interest in all things worldly?

And then one day, my friend told me that this Ashram was the place where I could be redeemed. She thought it was in my best interest and three days after landing here, I am still wondering if it was so.

* * *

Vandana had damp eyes. She held my hand and pressed it as if to comfort me. But Swamiji's expressions didn't change even once. He still had that warm, tranquil smile he had always had. This was the first time I was recreating and stringing aloud everything after it had happened. Until now, my focus had been to not to think about all this. And suddenly, I felt so much lighter, having blurted it out.

I stared at Swamiji. What will his perspective on things be? Will he have some good tips for me, or maybe he would tell me how I should meditate and what would work for me. The room got pregnant with anticipation for his words. And then he opened his mouth.

'Good job, Samar. Go now. It's time for *Karma* Yoga,' he said.

I gaped at him with an open mouth. I just did something I never thought I ever would. I went through the painful process of unfurling my past and he had no comments?

What an anticlimax.

Like a Melody Gone Wrong

The next day, I entered Swamiji's *kutiya* with lesser expectations. His actions were hard to predict. Again today, when we reached, he was deep in a meditative state. He had drifted to a different world and acted like that.

'The *karma* of a yogi,' he began to say as if we had never left last evening, 'is to be at absolute peace with himself and his surroundings. Have you ever wondered why all great souls have a constant faint smile on their faces?'

'Why?' Vandana asked.

'That's because they have seen it all. Nothing that happens around them surprises them. They know that we get life just once and spending such huge portions of it on troubles every day isn't worth it. Hence the constant smile. And to be at peace with yourself, it's very important to have a positive frame of mind. Today, we will work towards that. It is a pretty simple exercise. Will you do it with me?'

Vandana and I nodded our heads.

'Sit in proper *padmasana* and close your eyes. And now, tighten and relax your whole body, one body part at a time.'

We did as he instructed.

'Now imagine yourself on a small hill, with greenery all around. There is a pleasant wind blowing through your hair. Fragrance of ambrosia occupies your olfactory senses. You can listen to euphonious sounds of birds tweeting. Your body is relaxed and at complete rest.'

He paused for effect. I realized I could *feel* every word he was saying. My body had really travelled to the place he was describing.

'Now breathe out anger. Keep on breathing. And with these angry thoughts, you are throwing out all the negative thoughts you have in your body. Keep on breathing angrily. You are detoxing your body as you do that. Keep on breathing angrily.'

'Now think of the most affable person you can think of. Think of his or her face. Samar, imagine if she were to come in front of you on this mountain, what is the most heart-warming thing she can say to you? Think of what is the best thing you can say to her. Think of her smell. Think of how she looked. Think of how her touch felt.'

I heard every word he said. And imagined everything he said. It was like I was travelling through a marooned subway with an alternating electric red and pale yellow light. I could see the silhouette of a girl standing at the end of it. I started running faster and as I got nearer, the blinding light gave way to a face. And finally, I could see who she was. It hit me too hard. I opened my eyes with a jerk, stood up and stormed out of the *kutiya* immediately without taking permission to leave from Swamiji. I walked swiftly to my room and laid down on my bed with my head rooted deeply into the pillow. After the few minutes' numbness, I tried sorting my thoughts.

I didn't have a right to think of anyone but Kanika.

Then where did *her* thoughts come from? With every sentence that came out of Swamiji's mouth, it was her image, her touch, her smell that I remembered.

It was Navya Sharma.

* * *

I met Navya in Goa when I ran away, like a bird one could not cage. I met her when I lived under the delusion that Kanika had cheated on me.

Incidentally, the *Karma* Yoga today was to clean the corridors with the wiper. This is what I had done in Goa for a living. Circumstances were throwing me back in time, exactly what I was trying to leave behind. Dinner was to be followed by washing our own utensils, which was another thing I had been doing in Goa.

Before I slept off, I counted the numbers of hours left to see Swamiji again. Swamiji definitely had the power to stir up thoughts and mirror reflections. For better or worse, I could not say then.

* * *

When Swamiji asked Vandana and me to sit in front of him, I had a bunch of questions in my head. Why was he giving birth to such profoundly hitting emotions in me? What had he inferred and was he leading me to the right direction? Swamiji, with the same serene smile that he always wore, looked at me.

'Samar, you are definitely a good student. I am not saying this because you listen intently in your lectures but because you feel yoga when you do it.'

I knew he was referring to my extreme reaction yesterday.

'You have the focus and the mental strength. The only thing missing is peace within your mind and body.

I nodded and he paused for effect.

'And now you would have to tell us about what you were thinking yesterday.'

There was no way I was telling that to him. He was Swamiji and I respected him a lot and I wanted to be treated for mental unrest but this was something different. Navya was too personal a memory for me to share it with anyone. And honestly, I couldn't muster courage to even disburse the news to Swamiji. And once again, I could bet on Swamiji observing every knit on my eye brow and reading every thought in my mind.

'Would you want to hear a story, Samar?' he asked.

I nodded.

'I want to tell you the story of Jagdish. His mother and his friends used to call him Jaggi. His father was a carpenter in Allahabad. Jaggi had three sisters. His father was a happy man and he used to infuse his cheery aura around. The family lived together in a small slum.

But things began to go wrong when tuberculosis started consuming his father. Two years later, his youngest sister was killed by a car while she was crossing the road. People died all the time in that slum so the neighbours didn't care too much. But if one were to zoom in, the family stood devastated. Jaggi's mother tried but couldn't earn much. So, at a tender age of twelve, Jaggi became the sole bread earner of his family. His growth had to be accelerated and he decided to dedicate the rest of his life to his family. He didn't marry till he had married off all his sisters. Until one day, when he woke up three things hit him.

Firstly, his mother had silently passed away in her sleep that morning in her sleep. She was sixty five, which was normally considered a full age to die in the locality. She wasn't excessively healthy anyway.

Secondly, now that all his sisters were married and his mother was not there, he was alone in the house.

Thirdly, it was his thirty fifth birthday. His male friends, the few of them that were there, had families which kept them busy. With his sisters and mother gone, and having never cared about his own marriage, he was more lonely than he had ever imagined he could be.

He felt extremely depressed about the way his life had turned out. It was as if he had woken up every single morning, trying his best to survive the day without starving. He sat and thought about what he wanted to achieve in life, what would be his goal now. And when he couldn't come up with anything, he got even more depressed.

So once the condolence meetings and cremation of his mother were done, he locked his house from outside and couriered the key to his elder sister. And took a bus and made way to Rishikesh. Misery has a suction pull which could be ten times powerful than that of gravity. It is so easy to fall into depression but it takes courage to free oneself from its diabolic clutches.

In case you've not figured out till now, I am Jagdish. And this is the first time my name has been pronounced inside the borders of this Ashram. There is no pain I haven't felt or I can't understand, Samar. I could be your doctor. Open up. Tell me what is bothering you.'

I knew that a lot of pain existed in the world and that I wasn't the only one who was a victim of those dire happenings but for the first time ever it pinched me. I felt inferior, my pain felt trivial.

* * *

We meet a lot of people in life. Some register in our heads while others come and go without us taking notice. Navya was somebody whom everyone ended up taking notice of.

It's not about the fact that Navya was not a regular girl. A lot of girls are not regular girls. It was about the fact that you had one glance at her and you knew that there was something different about her, as if those matured and sombre expressions were struggling to fit onto her delicate face. Her sharp jutting collar bones and conspicuously strained veins of the neck almost looked unforgiving. Her eyes were steady but her walk, carefree. Her shoulders, unlike all shoulders around her, seemed unaffected by forces of gravity. Navya Sharma. Raised in Indore, Madhya Pradesh, the heart of India.

Navya used to have huge crushes on the authors Charlotte Bronte and Terry Pratchett, although belonging to very different eras and genres, they appealed to the person she was. She quit her pharmacy college in Bhopal and ran away to Goa for a more thrilling life. Tags weren't something she gave weightage to, so adventurous or escapist, she didn't care much. She loved mornings and often didn't sleep all night to watch the sun rise. She pretends that she understands politics but quickly confesses that she doesn't know shit. She's complicated to the outer world but to herself, she is simple and consistent. She is bad at many things too. She forgets things and it'll be difficult to tell apart her room from that of six careless boys. Her phone often gets disconnected for days when she doesn't pay the bill.

I met her at nineteen. Before me, she dated a shopkeeper in Indore, who had a fashion retail store, and was bald had an ugly paunch but could talk about women brands with the air of a fashion magazine editor. She loved to move on. That was her gift. And most will say her curse too. She got bored too easily and lost interest quickly than most people.

When the first time I had seen her, she was visibly drunk. As she came closer to me, she flashed the unlit cigarette, asking me for a lighter. And the next thing I knew, she bent her head forward and puked all over my shoe.

She was different in every way imaginable. The way she looked at everything, the way she thought, the way she spoke, everything was unique. The way she did things. The way she was more talented than anyone her age. The way she looked: pretty, understated, unkempt.

I had met Navya in Goa, when I had been working there.

The place was called Woodstock Village. It was a shack in Arambol in North Goa. She was a guest there and I was the janitor, the chef, the manager, or anything that the shack required me to be.

When I carried her to her room after she puked on my shoe, the first words she said to me was, 'Aren't you going to kiss me?'

I disliked her then. It was instant and easy to not identify with the person she was. What was difficult was to hate her for long.

In the beginning, she didn't like me either. The second time we met, she got me beaten up by some bouncers. And that would have been the lowest point of most people's life. But I had seen much worse before and after that.

We learn something from everyone we meet. I think I've learnt more from Navya than from anyone else. She taught me it's not unavoidable to do what everyone else is doing. She was somebody who made her decisions on her own. Her parents wanted her to study Pharmacy in Bhopal. She had instead run away to Goa to spend some time there.

In Goa, she earned money enough to sustain herself by selling her paintings. But her real love was books. She loved reading and collecting books. Literature always remained her first love. It was her religion.

She taught me that it's important to follow one's dream. And yet, I had to tell her to follow her own dream, to become a writer, and that it was actually not that difficult.

She always maintained a stoic exterior, her facial expressions impervious to any kind of interpretation. She was an enigma, a mystery, which never really gave away, and chose to stay wound up.

She had a few turquoise highlights on her black hair which playfully kissed her high cheek bones. She commanded attention wherever she went. She just had to speak to win hearts.

And she could see through me. She could see what others were blind to. It was visible that I was not the guy who runs a shack in Goa and earns fifty rupees a day. But she loved to psychoanalyze me; it simultaneously induced awe and antipathy for her. She once quoted Ayn Rand to me, saying that a man will always be attracted to the woman who reflects his deepest vision of himself, the woman whose surrender permits him to experience a sense of self-esteem. His choice will always be a sum of his fundamental convictions.

We went on endless walks on the infinitely beautiful beaches in Goa. We used to chat until sunrise and I can never forget the hug she once gave me. Those walks, those talks, were some of the most the most soothing memories I had stacked in my heart.

She seemed incapable of undergoing as stable and strong an emotion as love, and yet, she said she was falling for me. She told me so. And that, I think, made everything fall apart. I really liked her but it almost seemed blasphemous to substitute Kanika. I couldn't reciprocate her feelings.

One random day, I woke up and I found her leaving Woodstock Village, without leaving a trace of where she was going. She went back to the same crowd she had come from. And that was the last I ever heard of her.

A few days after that, Kanika landed in Woodstock. Life got busy again, so I didn't think much of her. But now that Swamiji had reminded me of her, she was definitely a pleasant past memory. She was the melody gone wrong.

* * *

'You smile spanned the entire story,' Swamiji remarked as soon as I was done narrating.

'As I said, she was a pleasant memory.'

'Tell me Samar, when I say the phrase 'best friend,' who comes to your mind?'

I thought of the out-of-place question and after much thinking, I told him that there was no name which came to my mind. If I really had to take a name, it would be Saloni.

'Samar,' Swamiji continued, 'a balanced life has several elements. To have your head in place and mind at peace,' Swamiji said, 'you need to have a balance of all these elements. Your mind and body have been disturbed for several months now because you lost the person you loved the most. And before you want to do anything in life, you need to bring that element of yours at complete peace.'

I was looking down, sitting in a relaxed cross legged posture. I looked up at him with pleading eyes, 'What do you mean Swamiji?'

'I mean you are lonely, Samar. You need a companion. You need a . . . *friend.* And it's not easy making a new friend at this juncture for you. Your mind isn't ready for that yet. What you need is someone who knows where you have been, someone in front of whom you are not conscious of making an impression, who knows who you are and what you stand for.'

'And you think Navya is that person?'

'She definitely does seem to be.'

I thought about what he had just said. I had several doubts. On one hand, I had no idea where Navya was. Finding her out will be a task in itself. Let's say I do manage to find her; what do I tell her then? I was still too emotionally unavailable to be in love with her, I reasoned. So I put in so much effort to find someone whose love I can't reciprocate. And then, when she gets comfortable with me again, I tell her that I still don't love her?

It didn't make sense to me.

Swamiji's eyes had magical powers and from the way he looked at me, it seemed he was aware of every single apprehension in my head.

'I know your doubts Samar. When you will meet her, it will either go well or go wrong. But it's absolutely essential for you to find out what it will be. I will help you prepare for it in the next three days. There are three things I want to tell you. There are things you need to know as a young man. You wouldn't understand or appreciate them immediately. But you will understand them eventually. I can only hope that they will add clarity in your head and conviction in your step. Go and rest now in your room and meet me tomorrow.'

I left the *kutiya*. But Vandana decided to stay over.

It seemed there was something on her mind she wanted to discuss with Swamiji.

'Are you sure that they should meet again? Maybe it's best that both of them have moved on,' she asked him.

'If I understand Navya at all, just like Samar, she is also living in imbalance. They are two unstable souls, if they would come together, they would unite in no time.'

'But what if they don't?'

'Then nobody knows what will happen to Samar. But it's a risk which we just need to take.'

* * *

Embrace Who You Are

I waited for Vandana the next day and once she came, we exchanged smiles and entered the *kutiya*. I had very high expectations today.

'Samar, I want you to start. Tell me *now*, what is bothering you?' he asked the same question he had asked me the first time we had met.

'Swamiji, my problem is that I can't control my mind. I think it just leads me anywhere and these days, and it's usually not a very comfortable place. I need to learn to control it better. And I have no idea how to do it.'

'You're saying you can't control your mind?'

'Yes Swamiji.'

'Samar, once there was a man riding a horse. He met a traveller on his way.

The traveller asked the horse rider, 'Where are you going?'

The horse rider replied, 'Why are you asking me? Ask the horse!'

'Your mind is like the horse. And you are the one riding it, Samar. You have to take it wherever you want to take it. Nobody is born with excellent riding skills. It is acquired and mastered over time, with experience. Not only that, once you've learnt how to ride the horse, you have to learn to guide it with responsibility too.'

It took me a good few minutes to process and absorb the information. How could he compress such overwhelming advice in such a few statements? And then I realized what my shortcoming was.

'Swamiji, I understand you view,' I said. 'But the challenge is that how does one learn to ride this horse?'

'What would you do if it were a real horse which you had to climb?'

'Well, I would struggle to climb it and would keep on struggling till I managed to climb it successfully.'

He smiled. And I knew I had answered my own question.

'I want to teach three things to both of you in the next three days. As I said, you won't understand them when you hear them first, but as and when you do assimilate, you will make peace with yourself.'

Vandana and I listened intently. We felt as if we were going to hear very important words in the next few minutes.

'The first thing is that you need to *stop trying to be somebody else and embrace who you are.*'

'It is futile trying to be a person whom you are not because the world doesn't care about what you are running from. You need to stop doing that embrace yourself with your shortcomings. Your imperfections are as much a part of you, as your perfections are. It's easy to embrace the perfections. What is challenging is embracing your imperfection.'

Swamiji beamed at us and listened to him with rapt attention.

'You are thinking that whatever I am saying makes complete sense. In fact, at some level, you might have known this already. But then, it's easier said than done. You're wondering as to how you'd go about doing it. That is where I am going to give you a *mantra*.'

'From now on, whenever negative thoughts cloud your mind, I want you to start paying attention to every thought crossing your mind. I mean, I want you to be *aware* of what is going through your mind at that time. Slowly and gradually, as you will get more and more conscious of what's going through your mind, you will start gaining control over your mind. You will feel it yourself. It's a slow process. But it's the only process there is.'

It sounded a pretty simple thing to do. In fact, it seemed so simple that one could wonder what good will it do. And I think it might have shown on my face.

'Samar,'' Guruji spoke, 'I want you to do a simple exercise for me.'

'*Ji* Guruji.'

'For ten seconds, focus on your breath. Just one cycle, breathe in and breathe out.'

I did as he said. And then again, my bewilderment might have shown on my face.

'What you did just now was equivalent to picking a dumbbell once and keeping it back. One might think what good would it do? But if you go to a gym daily, and lift that dumbbell as a routine, you start seeing changes in your body. That is what I want you to do with your brain. And slowly, you will perceive the transformation.'

He wanted us to pay attention to what we were paying attention to. And then, in my head, it began to add up and make sense, at least theoretically. I began to think of benefits this could have.

- It would mean we would pay complete attention to what we were doing and have lesser distractions because we would be aware of the distraction
- It meant we would be calmer because we will actively block any unpleasant thoughts
- It meant we would be happier because we will actively build upon happy thoughts

This is what went through my head, while I was still sitting in front of him, looking at him. The session ended there. Vandana and I came out, in a rather silent state. And without exchanging any words, we retired to our respective rooms. I was too preoccupied throughout the session to think what was going through her head.

* * *

As I stood in the corridor outside my room on the first floor, I could see the complete Ashram. The thing about The Ashram was that nothing *ever* changed there. Even the people didn't change much. The same Panditji would sit in the temple porch. The same receptionist. The same calm atmosphere of the place. The same secluded *kutiya* in one corner.

Panditji was meditating in unruffled silence. I saw him and felt jealous. On the face of it, it seemed so simple. He came, sat down, crossed his legs, closed his eyes, kept his palms on his knees, enchanted some mantras and attained absolute peace with himself. But in reality, this was the toughest thing to do and if you could do this, rest was much easier.

I had only one problem. That the more I thought about Navya, the more positive my thoughts got. She became a goal for me; almost like something to look forward to after a tiring day at work. But, every time her thoughts came into my head, they were inevitably be followed by a pang of guilt. Yeah, because of Kanika. Just then, Swamiji came to my mind.

Stop trying to be somebody else and embrace who you are.

I realized I should stop thinking about what Panditji is doing. If meditation has to come to me, it will come when the time comes. And there have been way too many people in this world, who have lived a fruitful life, without even being aware of the concept of meditation.

And the second thing was that if my mind wanted me to think of Navya, I should let it. If I want to relive some of my memories, it was okay. If Navya had been there standing with me at that moment, she would have looked around and ridiculed them saying, 'Peace doesn't come from all this drama. It just comes from being loved, feeling loved. Or maybe just from doing your work. This is like pushing against a wall, manually. While the right way is to just go around the wall and keep walking.'

She would have gone up to the Panditji, who was deep into meditation and poked him in the nose or something. She definitely wouldn't have seen the halo around Swamiji's *kutiya* and she would have just walked in, and said 'What's up' or something. She would have made the place go crazy.

Once she suddenly had the craving to play with a balloon at nine in the night. Without luck, we searched around for it in the small market in Goa. In the end, she went into a chemist store and bought a condom. She tore apart the packet, blew it and tied a knot. Her balloon was ready.

That was exactly what I needed. I needed some crazy in my life.

Not Immediately, But Definitely

The second day was no less unnerving. My only worry was that Swamiji might ask me what I comprehended of what he said yesterday. The truth was that even though I understood the literal meaning of his words, I knew I was a long way from completely experiencing what he was saying. But thankfully, there were no questions, no viva-voce. Typical Swamiji.

'Samar, once again, I will start with you. Tell me, what do you think of meditation?'

Honestly, I had always been and still was a non-believer in meditation. But I was sitting in The Ashram, with Swamiji, who must be a great proponent of this art. I mean, it is a little difficult to go to the Pope and say you're an atheist, right?

'I still don't understand this concept, Swamiji,' I confessed.

Swamiji nodded, as he already knew that I was a nonbeliever.

'So here is what I want you to do. I want you to not meditate any more. This Ashram is good only for teaching you the technique of meditation which I'm sure you've learnt by now.'

I was bemused. Swamiji had said the exact opposite of what I had expected him to say. There was one thing constant about being with him. He kept surprising you with his teachings.

'Then wouldn't I be wasting whatever I have learnt here?' I asked.

'No. What you need to understand Samar is that it is okay to be wrong sometimes. If the idea of meditation doesn't appeal to you, you need not do it because you're being told to do so. You're a twenty one year old boy. So relax, bunk a few classes, smash some glasses, break your wrist, play in the sun and dip in the sea. Don't be harsh on yourself.'

'What if it never comes to me?' I asked.

'Then I would believe perhaps you were right in being a nonbeliever in meditation. But, if it is me reading the signs; one day, you will have so much going through your head that you would have to sit down, close your eyes and tackle one thought at a time. And meditation would seem like the best option.'

It could happen and it could not. I left it on circumstances and destiny and took Swamiji's leave for the day.

Vandana, however, decided to stay back. She must have been taken aback by the flouting of Yoga and meditation rules Swamiji just proposed.

'Vandana *behen*,' Swamiji said, 'Samar is a very depressed fellow. And I can see that meditation is only going to prove destructive to him. When you already have so many negative thoughts and you close your eyes and sit in a pensive mode, I'm afraid meditation would only amplify those thoughts, probably make them echo in the head. Which is what seems to be happening in his case.

Even though Samar is both strong and sensible, I believe we cannot rule out self harm he could do in the situation he is in right now.

* * *

I didn't sleep well that night. My head felt cluttered with all that I had learnt in these two days. It went against everything my parents, teachers and elders had been preaching since childhood.

A part of me believed that this whole institution of The Ashram, Swamiji, meditation, yoga, introspection was a sham and that I was being misled.

Another part of me believed that things were finally falling in place. That I was on the right path and I should thank my stars for having led me here.

I was confused, clueless and sleepless.

* * *

If I understood everything correctly, this was going to be my final day with Swamiji. Today, Vandana was already inside when I arrived five minutes early.

'Samar, today is your final day at The Ashram. I want you two to start your journey tomorrow morning.'

'Both of us?!' Vandana said.

'Yes. Both of you. I want both of you to make this journey. You will start your journey tomorrow, to look for Navya, wherever she is in this country.'

'*Ji* Swamiji,' both of us said. And looked at him with anticipation for our final lesson.

'The final thing I want to say to you is another very simple idea. And as I told you on the first day, it's like lifting a heavy weight. You have to practice it every single day, several times to benefit from it. But the benefit is worth the pain. And soon, it stops seizing to be a pain and becomes a part of you.'

'It's a very simple thing to do. Samar and Vandana, I want you to help every single person in this world you possibly can. There'll be two ramifications of it: Firstly, that person will feel nice and become your friend. And secondly, and more importantly, you will feel good and a lot of your doubts will begin to melt away. This is the strength you need. Slowly, it will become a part of your nature. Your joys will be sweeter and tough times will become rarer. All said and done, this, from now on, should become the mantra of your life: Share your joys, and work towards decreasing others sorrows. Can you two do this for me?'

Vandana and I nodded fervently. I knew it was really easy to sit in that *kutiya* and nod our heads. But it will be much tougher to actually put it into practice. We will be faced with difficult questions, situations and will have to make difficult choices.

Swamiji looked at me straight into the eye, as if he was passing some energy through the root of the eyes. And it was that invisible, intangible energy which told me that I was ready. At least in theory, I had learnt everything I needed to learn. And now, I could only rest my full faith in Swamiji's words.

* * *

As I stepped out, once again, Vandana stayed on, and had another conversation with Swamiji I would get to know about much later.

'You want me to go with him?' Vandana asked.

'Yes. I do.'

'As much as I would love to make this journey with him, I would still want to know why you want me to go with him.'

'That is because I have a feeling that your inner peace lies somewhere on the way to the search of his inner peace. Sure, your destinations are different but your journeys have a big overlap.'

Key To My Inner Peace

It was the seventh of June which meant I had just spent a week at the Ashram.

We got up and decided to go for the morning yoga session, just to say bye to everyone for the final time. Even though I had been prepared, Vandana had been caught off guard as Swamiji had told her just one day before.

By the time the session ended, the taxi was already waiting outside. I was once again reminded of how popular Vandana was and how unknown I still was.

I thought of Navya. We were taking a train to Bhopal to look for her and I tried to think what I felt for her. Was it just friendship? Was I ready to be romantically inclined towards someone?

I had mixed feelings about this trip. I had never thought I would go looking for Navya, partially because I thought it was best to part ways with her and partially because I had no idea where she was in Bhopal.

All I knew about Navya was –

- She was in a college in Bhopal
- It was a Pharmacy college. I had faint recollection of the name. Something like Acropolo or something

– She was from Indore and that's where her family
   was

I saw Vandana sitting beside me, enjoying her groundnuts. Her uniqueness as a person kept baffling me from the moment I saw her. She didn't talk like most forty year olds. She didn't dress up like them. She was more vibrant, mischievous and liked to get into trouble. Along with Swamiji, she became my confidant too and I still hadn't gotten the chance to decrypt her. I don't know whether she had begun to be less annoying or I had gotten used to her annoying ways. Anyway, we reached the station in an hour.

On seeing around, we thought of the promise we made to Swamiji. We got started with the job. We helped people find their platforms, pick their luggage, bought small packets to chips for the beggars, pushed the wheel chairs of old people. We kept at it until it was time for our train to leave. And we did it with a smile.

And exactly three minutes before the departure time of the train, Vandana and I met in front of our bogie. She was gasping for breath from the hard work, and took a breather standing close to the entrance before we entered the bogie.

And then it hit us. The *high* of helping people. This was the feeling Swamiji was talking about. This was what he wanted us to pursue when he told us to help people.

As we stood there, Vandana turned around and went and picked a light fiction read from one of the book stalls at the Railway Station. I must have given her a judgemental look.

'What? Can't I like to read light fiction by a young author?'

'You sure can,' I said, mellowing my condensation.

As I began to enter, she held my arm and told me to wait.

'Don't you see who's in your coach before you enter?'

'Why would I?' I replied.

'What sort of a twenty one year old are you? Don't you check if there's any girl in the bogie?'

'No. I don't. What's the point? I have full faith in myself. I can never talk to strangers.'

'Then you're in good luck young man because that happens to be an area I specialize in,' Vandana said.

'We are going to meet Navya. Do you really think I should be chatting up to women of my age on this train?'

'It's not like you're going to talk to the girl with an ill intention. Let's do it strictly for learning purposes. See, here is an eighteen year old girl, sitting right opposite your seat.'

'I don't believe in train romances. And anyway, she is travelling with her mom and dad. Two more people have the same surname in the bogie.'

Vandana gave me a swaggering smile, as if she knew something that I didn't.

'You can make any situation work in your favour. See, if she's with her parents and everything, you will have to get their confidence first.'

'And how does one do that?' I asked with disdain.

'Well, she's eighteen years old, so she must be about to enter college. So throw some buzz words. If she's from commerce, tell them you're from SRCC. If she is into science, tell her you're from a big shot Engineering college and concoct a bit about the admission procedures. Then her parents would want her to take *gyaan* from you.'

As I entered, I saw a dusky girl, who seemed unusually chirpy. She had two different coloured bracelets dangling from her left arm and other pieces of junk accessories hanging around her neck and ears. I exchanged a smile with her parents and tried to not be too friendly with her as that might be considered flirting.

We established a nice and congenial environment. Aunty wanted my lower berth to which I happily conceded. Upper births guarantee you privacy. Uncle offered me food which I accepted. The Physics HC Verma book in her hand told me that the girl was preparing for her Engineering exams. I happened to point out that the newer edition of the book was more extensive in terms of competitive examination question bank. So her mother, seemingly impressed, asked me the inevitable question. And I answered saying that I was a student of Delhi College of Engineering.

The evening went on, and I ended up having a longish chat with the girl about entrance exams and other usual things. The girl gave away her awe by her expressions and gestures. To be honest, I could have asked for her phone number. But I definitely had other things on my mind. I was supposed to look for the girl who held the key to my inner peace.

* * *

All this while I hadn't been thinking about the repercussions of my meeting with Navya: What if it becomes extremely awkward; What if she is with someone else now? How will I explain my sudden resurgence in her life?

Vandana and I got off the train and took an auto. And I got to see the first sights of Bhopal and it looked pleasant.

Vandana assumed we would check into a hotel but I had something else on my mind. I *needed* the internet, not just to check my mails and things but to do my primary research on Navya. The auto guy took us to a cyber café where I Googled for Pharmacy Colleges in Bhopal. There was one called Acropolis Institute of Pharmacy. I connected the vague Arcopolo I remembered. This was it. I noted the address.

I looked at Vandana. She didn't seem very presentable. Even I wasn't looking all that great. We needed cleaning up.

It was late afternoon already.

We were in Bhopal, and we didn't know anyone in the city. Looking for a room was a pain. Thankfully, I had yatra.com app on my phone. I browsed through the hotels on it and narrowed down on one, which was both, in my budget and comfortable enough. Whoa, all it took was a few seconds.

We checked into a nominal guest house. By the time we were done with the shower, it was almost three. If we really pushed ourselves, we could make it before the Administrative Department would close. Bhopal can't be a big city.

'Let's go,' I said.

But Vandana didn't seem interested in going anywhere that day. In fact, she convinced me to do it tomorrow.

'So what are we going to do today?' I asked Vandana.

'Is that even a question?'

'What do you mean?'

'Can't you see what we have in our room?' she said, salivating with excitement.

'What?'

'We have a TV! God, how badly I missed watching TV in the Ashram. All my Tulsi, Mihir, Kumolika must be missing me so badly. For the whole day today, I am not leaving this room,' she said, with the broadest grin I had ever seen on her.

Because of her unusual contour, I had forgotten that she was a forty year old Indian woman before anything else. And an Indian woman is incomplete without her TV serials. She tuned into Star Plus. I had to retreat to the balcony because I couldn't stand the jarring sight of that scene, which was getting repeated, with Sanskrit mantra chorus on loop in the background. But even standing in the balcony, I could hear high-pitched sobs from the speakers.

* * *

The next morning, even though we reached the college campus at ten itself, I chose to enter the Administrative Block at eleven. I was nervous about this and didn't want to take any chances.

We entered the office and looked around. We decided to go to the first table and asked them where we could see student's records. The person pointed to a table alongside.

Vandana had taken a long shower today and was wearing a brown *salwaar kameez*. She looked much neater and presentable.

I knew it was important to act confident in front of the officer. So I went and took a chair in front of the officer who was struggling with his computer. And looked at him confidently. Vandana followed suit.

'Sir, we needed a favour.'

'Yes?'

'We needed class and roll number of one person from your database,' I said.

'Can I know the purpose?'

'Well, actually she is a friend of mine.'

'Oh is it? Then why don't you know her class?'

'I never asked her. And she never told me.'

'Oh okay. Where did you meet her?'

'I met her in Goa. In Arambol actually.'

'What were you doing there?'

'I used to do run small errands, like cleaning the floor, scrubbing the utensils etc.'

'And what was she doing there?'

'She was a guest.'

'And what do you do in life generally?'

'I am an Engineering student from Delhi '

'Then what were you doing in Goa?'

'Well, I was running away from my girlfriend.'

'You think I am an idiot, don't you?'

'No sir. I think you are quite smart . . . and helpful.'

'Will you leave yourself or would I have to call the security?'

'We will leave ourselves,' I said and got up from the seat. Vandana gave me a plain look. I had messed up the conversation big time.

Lesson learnt: Honesty isn't always the best policy.

Vandana and I walked out of the Administrative Block and we saw the canteen in front of us. We went and took a table. I couldn't help looking at every passing girl, hoping it was her. I thought somebody like her was likely to be famous.

'Do you know someone called Navya Sharma?' I asked a bunch of guys sitting next to me. They gave me a blank look and shook their heads.

'Can you tell me where the Pharmacy Block is?'

They guided us to a grey building. I read sign boards and we reached the second year class, where I believed she should have been. A lecture was going on, so we decided to wait for it to get over. And when it did get over, my eager eyes looked all over for her face. I went inside the hall and saw all the remaining faces, but she was nowhere. I went and checked the first year and the third year as well, but with no luck. I asked people if they knew someone called Navya Sharma. Nobody had heard the name.

'Now what should we do?' I asked Vandana.

'Let's go back to the canteen and sit. Maybe, we would spot her there.'

'Navya wasn't the canteen type,' I said.

'Then what type was she?'

'Chilling in her room and doing her own stuff type.'

'I don't think we can check that, can we?'

We walked dejectedly to the canteen, when Vandana saw some books in a student's hand.

'I have an idea. Come,' she said, and got up.

'But where . . .'

'She took me to the librarian. None of the books would have accumulated dust if the librarians were usually pretty.

Because then the guys, on the pretext of hitting on them, would take unnecessary help of these librarians (and have kids with them in their heads).'

'You see her?' Vandana asked me.

'Yes. I do. So?'

'You need to trap her'

'What does that mean? Listen, the one thing I cannot do is walk up to a woman and generate a conversation out of thin air.'

'Samar, you remember when I told you that I help my guy friends talk to women?'

'No,' I lied.

'Well, I think you can really use my superior knowledge at this stage,' she said, and kicked started a completely random rant on how a girl's brain works and how a guy can use that to his advantage.

I wasn't fully convinced but I decided to give in because of the effort she put in her speech. We went to the fiction section and zeroed on Harry Potter. And with the book in my hand, I walked up to the librarian.

'Hey, wanted your opinion on one thing. I want to give a book to my nine year old niece, you think 'Harry Potter and the Philosopher's Stone' is a good pick?'

The girl's eyes twinkled a little. Unquestionably, she was a Potter fan. 'Oh yes, definitely. You will be introducing her to a world that she will cherish forever.'

And then, I looked at her closely as if there was something really interesting about her face.

'Has anyone told you that your nose wiggles just a little when you smile,' I said.

'No? Does it?' she smiled a little more.

'See! You did it again! Looks so darn cute!'

The librarian hadn't had too many compliments thrown at her. And when I swooped in, with a genuine and natural sounding conversation, she took me on face value, and we were friends.

'Hey listen, there is this book that I am looking for. But it has already been taken by a girl. Can you look up your database and help me find her?'

She looked left and right and luckily there was no one nearby. That was a good sign. It meant she wanted to help.

'Tell me her name, quickly.'

'Navya Sharma.'

She typed the name and I looked carefully to check that she got the spelling right. Her computer processed as I looked on with great anticipation. I felt as if I was just one step away from finally tracing Navya.

'Well, actually, I am sorry; we haven't ever had a student called Navya Sharma,' she said.

I was distressed. I felt as if it had all been a lie. She was not from this college. God knows whether she was from Indore or not. I felt convinced that she was phony. All the excitement and positivity which had built up in the last week was shattered in that moment. The inertia of the moment made me hate my time at The Ashram too.

All this while when I had not been looking for Navya, she remained a pleasant memory. But now, Swamiji had taken away that happy part of my past; From now on, I would remember her as a liar.

I looked devastated and I could see it getting mirrored

in Vandana's eyes. As she looked on, with Swamiji's words repeatedly coming back to her.

If the meeting with Navya doesn't go well, it could shatter Samar really badly.

81

Such a Long Journey,
Such a Wrong Journey

Vandana booked the earliest ticket she could find to Delhi. She must have had some 'connection' because despite heavy rush, we were on the train the same day. And once again, Vandana bought a light romantic novel off the book store at the Railway Station. Books in her hands never went with the rest of her image.

As soon as we were in the train, she dug into the novel. She was unusually quiet today, as if she was reading the best novel she had ever picked. I was getting bored and naturally, wasn't in the best of moods after what I saw and experienced. What I needed was some conversation to keep me distracted and my head busy. And Vandana had the knack of doing exactly what annoyed me.

Once dinner was served in the train, I couldn't take it anymore. So I jumped off my berth and went up to hers. And I took the book from her hand.

'What time will the train reach Delhi tomorrow?' I tried to make small talk, snatching her book away.

'Eight thirty. And give that book to me.'

'What if I don't?'

'Why would you do that? I don't think you have read this kind of fiction in your whole life.'

'Perhaps I will start today,' I retorted. I would have done anything to stop my whirring head from ruminating then.

I settled in my berth and looked at the book in my hand. The book was called 'Love or nothing', which I thought was a weird title. The author's name was Nayanika Sharma.

I read half the book in two hours straight. This was some seriously talented stuff I was reading. I was interrupted by Vandana when she came to tell me that she was going to sleep and that I should express my gratitude to her for lending me the book. Within a few minutes, she was throwing loud snores at the whole cabin, and I was no longer the only one being annoyed at her.

I went back to the book. I felt a sudden curiosity to know about the author, Nayanika Sharma. I turned to the last page, which normally has the author's bio.

I sat up because of the surprise! I had told her that she should become an author. I had never thought she would take me so seriously and succeed at it so soon. It also answered several other questions.

It was her. It was Navya. Those eyes, those ears, that nose, that skin, that hair. I had found her. Or at least, the first real trace of her. I woke up Vandana, without making efforts to contain my excitement and thus earning angry glares from co-passengers.

'What happened?' she asked, as she sat up.

'We've found her! We've found her, Vandana.'

* * *

'You have a house in Delhi?' I asked Vandana.

'Yes, but do *you* have a house in Delhi?'

'Yes, I do. Earlier I had a roommate. Now I live there alone.'

We took a cab to my place in Rohini and we walked into my flat, which I had left just a few days ago. I didn't have many friends in this area and I decided to refrain from contacting them. Once we were inside and settled in, I picked up the book again to look for any clues of Navya's whereabouts.**

Nayanika Sharma is a pharmacy college dropout, who doesn't like to spend too much time in one place. She is nineteen years old, and plans to be a prolific painter, and write in her free time. She is presently in some part of India, where she can do what she wants, without being disturbed.

That was the weirdest bio I had ever read of a published author. It was as if Navya had written a bio telling as little about her as she could. But she hadn't lied about her college. But she didn't seem to have lied about anything other than her name; which was a mini relief. And, I guess you wouldn't really blame her for changing her name when she is living alone in Goa, doing things most parents will not approve of.

But the sad part was that even after having her book in my hand, I had no leads on how to look for her. I didn't even know which city she was in. And knowing her bizarre ways, she could be anywhere.

'So where do we start from?' I asked Vandana, who had been cursing me for not telling her before that there was no TV in my house.

**I had to continue calling her Navya. She was the girl I knew and interacted with. I could not switch to Nayanika, even though I came to know her real name.

'Give me the book,' she said, and studied it carefully. 'Let me spend some time with the book and look for some clues.'

I let her do it. Not that I had many options anyway.

I went to my room and Vandana went to the other when we reached home. I closed the door, switched to some loose pajamas. Then I sat on the floor, in *padmasana* and closed my eyes. I tried to concentrate on my breath in the beginning. And once the breath became regular, I took my brain back to the day I had met Navya for the first time. I concentrated hard to recall every minute I had spent with her and looked for any clue which would help me find her.

Navya had been a clever person. She had made sure there were no hints.

I was disturbed by a knock on the door by Vandana. She seemed excited. I could see she had an idea. As she entered the room, her eyes fell on my phone.

'Why has your phone been ringing continuously since morning? And why aren't you taking these calls?' she asked me.

'Well, actually it's my twenty first birthday today. People are calling to wish me.'

'Then why aren't you taking their calls?'

'I can't see a point. I don't feel any excitement for my birthday anymore.'

'Ouch,' Vandana made a face. 'Were you always like this?'

'Yes. I was always like this,' I lied. 'But you walked in with excitement. What's up?'

'Did you see the copyright page of the book? It had

85

the publisher's address. And it's here in Delhi. We can ask them for Navya's whereabouts.'

'Why couldn't I catch that?' I said.

Sometimes we are so busy staring at the closed door that we don't look for any other way out.

'We will tell them we are journalists. Journalists have access to everybody,' Vandana continued, almost breathless with excitement.

This plan had a real chance of working. I didn't want to waste any time. And within a few moments, we were in a cab to Panchsheel Park, where the publisher's office was. I really wanted the odds to be in my favour this time.

Searching for her

It was almost like seeing a Mc Donald's outlet empty; the publisher's office one such unbelievable anti-climax. We had expected a jazzy floor with lots of corporate looking busy people walking around. Instead, we came across a rather decrepit office, with a few old men sitting. To think that *these* were the people behind a fancy publishing company was a bit of a letdown.

The only female employee there was a girl in her mid-twenties. She was the front desk manager, who guided us to the room of the Managing Director. He was Anirban Basu. Those huge hipster specs didn't really compliment his dark and wrinkly face. Plus, if he weren't moving his mouth to chew whatever he was chewing, someone would have mistaken his red lips for a coat of rich lipstick.

We sat in front of him, and I let Vandana take charge.

'Sir, my name is Vandana Manchanda and I am a journalist. We are doing a cover story on the upcoming fiction writers in India and for that we wanted to interview Ms Navya Sharma. Also, we wanted to talk to you regarding the same.'

'What can I do for you in that respect?' Mr Basu said, coming straight to the point.

Sachin Garg

'Well, actually we needed her contact details.'

Mr Basu got a little alert when Vandana said that. For the first time he looked at us, scanned us from top to bottom.

'So are you from a newspaper or a magazine or TV channel?' Mr Basu asked.

Vandana and I didn't reply immediately. We looked at each other and then Vandana said, 'Newspaper.'

'Oh okay, I see. Which newspaper?' Mr Basu asked.

Vandana hesitated, and then after thinking for a second, she said, 'Hindustan Times.'

Mr Basu was an experienced businessman. These little hints, these pauses and the look we had on our faces, were more than enough pointers for him to know that we were bluffing.

'I am sorry, but Navya has given us strict instructions not to share her contacts with anyone.'

'Not even media people?' I asked.

'Especially the media people.'

The conversation was over from Mr Basu's side. It was time for us to leave.

He picked up the phone on his desk, and asked the receptionist to connect him to Jaaved Khan, who I knew was a famous author.

Vandana and I walked out of his cabin with our heads hung.

'Now what? I have no ideas whatsoever,' I said.

'Is it? I thought it was quite obvious.'

'Lady Buddha, please enlighten me too,' I said, sarcastically

'Did you notice he asked the receptionist to connect him to Jaaved Khan, the famous author?'

'Yes, so?'

'That means the receptionist has the database we require.'

'So? You think she will give it to us?'

'Samar, she is a woman and you keep forgetting my talent.'

'Of helping guys chat up girls? You think it will work on her? She isn't eighteen and gullible.'

She gave me her trademark wicked smile.

* * *

'Hi, what's your name?' I went to the receptionist and said condescendingly.

'Well, Aradhya. Why?'

'I am joining as Sales Manager. I am Samar Garg.'

She gave me a confused look, as she probably wondered why she had not been told that they were getting a new Sales Manager. Thankfully, she decided to play along.

'Oh hi,' she said, extending her hand.

'Well, ever since I walked in, I've noticed you've been sitting idle. So I was discussing stuff with Mr Basu and we decided that need to add more responsibilities to your profile.'

'It's nothing like that, sir,' she said, and went onto list whatever she had done in last one year to convince me that she was doing a lot. I was just waiting for her to be done.

'Well, that's okay. Also, I need to speak to some authors. And I am going to start with Mr Jaaved Khan and Navya Sharma. Give me their phone numbers.'

'Sure, sir,' she said and went back to her computer. She scribbled something on a piece of paper and gave it to me.

'But this is only Jaaved Khan. Where is Navya Sharma's number?'

'Sir, actually . . . she never shares her phone number. In fact, she keeps travelling and keeps changing her number. She is always quite hard to reach.'

'But it's important that I speak to her for marketing purposes. There must be some way to reach her?'

'Well, actually, whenever I've bumped into her outside work, she never used to be in her senses. She used to be high or something.'

'You mean like high on weed?'

'I don't think it was weed. It was something stronger. Someone told me what she does. I can't recollect the name of that substance right now.'

'LSD? Acid? Hash?' Vandana guessed.

'No. It was some drug I had never heard of. It sounded straight from the Chemistry lab.'

'Oh, I think I know what you are alluding to,' Vandana said.

'What?' Aradhya and I said in a chorus.

'Methamphetamine, right?'

'Yes! That was it!'

'How did you know that?' I asked Vandana.

'That's not important. Let's concentrate on Navya for now. You have any idea where can we find her?'

'Well, I know that her present boyfriend is DJ Vyk. So I think if you find out where he is playing, she should be easy to trace.'

So Navya had a boyfriend. On one hand, we had taken the next step towards finding Navya. On the other hand, she had gone a step away from me, as she now had a boyfriend. It hurt.

'Thanks, Aradhya. Tomorrow is my first day at work. I'll see you tomorrow,' I said and we left the publisher's office.

Vandana called for a cab to Rohini.

'So this is it,' I said.

'What do you mean?'

'I mean it's time we ended our quest. Navya has a boyfriend. She has moved on. I should move on too.'

'Shut up. We are not giving up at this stage. I know your generation. Boyfriends mean nothing today. Half of you are in relationships simply because it's fashionable to have a trophy around.'

'You really think Navya is like that after all that I have told you?'

'Samar, commitment is a huge delusion your generation is living today. It is a scam they unknowingly pull off every day. And for all you know, she has forced herself into it to stop thinking about you.'

'Whatever. I can't do it.'

You might think of Vandana either as a crack head or as a pure genius. But there was one thing about her: When she wanted to convince someone, she could convince people for anything.

We had a good long discussion on it, which soon turned into an argument. And yes, she convinced me to at least, go look for her, meet her and then give up if I still want to.

* * *

91

We came back to my flat. I didn't feel up for a conversation or any more research about the guy Navya had supposedly fallen in love with. I retired to my room and waited for Vandana to break into my room, once again. But she didn't come this time.

I saw the sun go down through the window. I was just lying on my bed doing nothing. Sometimes you *need* to blank out. Just exist, hang in there like a vegetable or blah, watching things happen without reacting or doing anything. That's what I was doing.

I got to see Vandana's excited walk only around eleven in the night.

'DJ Vyk is playing at a club called Urban Pind tonight.'

'Getting inside won't be a problem; go, get ready now!'

'I like the confidence Vandana, but I'm sorry. I'm not up for it this time.'

'Shut up and concentrate on getting into the best shirt you have,' she said and went back to her room. I heard the water dripping from the shower. She was taking it very seriously.

I looked into my cupboard after several weeks. In the right most corner, there was a maroon shirt I liked. Right below it was the white T-shirt I had bought in Goa after working extremely hard to earn the money for it.

I slipped into the maroon shirt and threw my hair under the tap. I had to put some gel in my hair to make them look civilized. I also shaved my stubble. I then ironed my favourite trouser and polished my shoes which had gotten dirty because of pure disuse.

I was hoping she wouldn't overdress.

Vandana came out wearing a neat and classy shirt with a trouser. Basically, she was sporting a corporate look. The list of unexpected and crazy things that Vandana did was unending.

'Today, we will look like a boss and subordinate from an MNC, who are hanging out after work.'

'Erm, okay, as you say,' I said, half thinking. Vandana looked at me, top to bottom and said, 'It's hard to tell in formals where does one come from. We are all corporate brothers.'

I looked at her a little more properly and I noticed that her style was not bad at all. For the first time I realized Vandana actually had a pretty body, as she was slim and quite well shaped for her age. I noticed a hint of make up on her face which made me realize that for forty year old, she had aged pretty gracefully.

'Come, stand next to me,' she said, as she stood in front of the mirror. 'Yes, I think we can pass off as being boss and subordinate.'

'So you think you and I can get through the personality check on the entrance of Urban Pind?'

'I am sure we can. Trust me, I have been there a few times,' she said with a plain face, leaving no clue that whether she was kidding or was serious.

Just then, someone rang our doorbell. Nobody used to ring our doorbells normally. But today, it was even more surprising for two reasons –

–   Nobody knew I was in Delhi and home.
–   It was eleven thirty in the night and an odd hour for someone to drop by unannounced.

I went and opened the door. A man in his late twenties was waiting. 'Your cab is waiting, sir,' he said.

* * *

We reached Urban Pind and got off the cab. I looked around and I saw impeccably polished faces; I bet they had bathed in a concoction of foundations and expensive perfumes. There was a bit of a fog around, but I think it was hookah smoke as it was the month of June.

'Let's go back Vandana. You have the cab driver's number? He wouldn't have gone far yet.'

'You sissy, here is what we will do. We will keep our chins high and as we will walk in, we will exchange a gentle smile with that guy who is wearing a black coat.'

'You think this will work?'

'No.'

It took a second for me to realize that she had said no instead of yes. It didn't do a lot of good to my confidence. But still, we gave it a shot. And it didn't work.

The bouncer told us it was an invites-only day at the club which was code for You-should-have-seen-yourself-in-the-mirror-and-invested-on-clothes-and-makeup-before-coming-to-a-posh-club.

'Now what?'

'I hate it when you say this 'now what', with a nasal twang like a helpless kid.'

'What option do we have?'

'You are fucking twenty one year old. Think of an option,' Vandana shouted at me. This was the first time I was seeing her get angry.

'The only option I can think of is to go back home and go to sleep.'

'From where I am seeing, that's not really an option.'

'Then you please guide me as to what you *do* see as an option,' I shouted back at her.

She gave me a disappointed look. And as I looked at her, she had a confused look on her face, as if she was thinking of something. Just then I saw in the backdrop there was a woman who was looking at her as if she knew her. She started approaching her and touched her on the elbow. Vandana turned around and looked at her as if she had seen the scariest ghost ever.

'What are you doing here?'

'I was praying to every God I believe in that I don't bump into you and look, what God has done,' Vandana said, with great dismay.

'There are one thousand clubs in Delhi. You mean to say you chose to come to Urban Pind and hoped not to see me? And you want me to believe that?'

'We had our reasons, Divya. Just help us get inside and please leave us alone.'

Divya didn't argue anymore and managed to somehow suppress her anger. She led us inside the club. As we followed her, this time nobody dared to stop us and instead the same bouncer smiled, nodded his head and welcomed us inside.

Who the hell was this Divya and what did Vandana have to do with her?

I'm Not That Guy

'How do you know this woman?' I shouted into Vandana's ear over the loud music. She decided to ignore my question. As we walked in, Divya was walking behind us. She escorted us to a table and started talking to the waiter. It was more than evident that she was telling him to take good care of us. I presumed it meant all the drinks were on the house.

I finally located him behind the DJ console and he really seemed to be enjoying his music. DJ Vyk: A relatively short and fair guy, sporting a beard style I had never seen before. And if those weren't the disco lights shining intermittently on his head, he had pink streaks with beads.

'After a round of three shots, I called for a Fresh Lime Soda. Divya was around all this while, keeping to herself; neither talking to me nor to Vandana. Finally, when she decided to disappear in the swarm, the awkwardness lurking in the air came to an end. Vandana was unsuccessfully trying to hide her bewilderment since the time we had bumped Divya. I had never seen her so winded.

She then spoke, breaking ten minutes of tedious silence between us, 'You will never know how thankful you should be for bringing you here.'

'I really am. Now can I ask what the hell was going on?'

'No.'

'Okay,' I said, deciding to let her be.

'I asked Divya about DJ Vyk. And she told me that Navya comes every time he plays. Earlier, she used to sit here on one fixed table. But after her book became viral, her readers kept disturbing her. So now she sits in some different corner every time.'

'By the way, that dude on the DJ console there is DJ Vyk,' she said. I had spotted him already, but I turned around to see him again.

DJ Vyk had several women around him and one could see he was quite sought after amongst the ladies. He seemed someone worthy of having Navya as a trophy girlfriend. He was good looking, successful and artistic. Where my best talent was making crystals in the chemistry lab; whom was I kidding?

'But where is Navya?' Vandana asked.

'I have no idea.'

'Let's take a walk around,' Vandana said and got up from where she was sitting.

We walked around the whole club looking for that face. But she was nowhere.

'I think you should call Divya again,' I suggested.

Vandana gave me an are-you-fucking-out-of-your-mind look.

So we decided to wait till DJ Vyk's performance got over and hoped that he would then go to meet her, and we will follow him.

We looked around: Everything was way too pretentious for us and we didn't bother comment on anybody. In

97

another life, I might have enjoyed the music or the skin show by the girls. But I was way too preoccupied that day.

DJ Vyk finished at two, after playing the-one-final-song three times, while we sat there discovering new threshold levels of our patience. He climbed the stairs and went upstairs. There was a door which we had passed by earlier without noticing, simply because it seemed way too unimportant. It seemed like one of those doors which lead to an abandoned garage or a secret huge junkyard. DJ Vyk entered the door and we followed behind him. Once we were inside, we realized that it was actually a VIP Lounge. The entrance might have been kept nondescript to keep it low key.

I stepped in, thinking of Navya. My heart was racing. This was it. Months of waiting and I was finally going to see her again. Will she recognize me? Will she be happy to see me? What were the chances that I will step in to see her lip locked with DJ Vyk's?

I looked around. There was more smoke that my nose could handle. Once my eyes got used to the smoke and the darkness, my eyes fell on the faces there. No one seemed human in that cabin. Some were lying around; like it was their bedroom and they had no energy. While others were snorting and injecting stuff like there was no tomorrow.

I noticed a syringe in the hands of a guy who had only half a body. And then, another guy took the same syringe and inserted whatever was remaining in that syringe in his veins. They were sharing a syringe, which meant that if one of them had AIDS, other would get it too. Once the second guy was done, he passed on the used syringe to a girl on his right, but she was too dazed out to notice.

And then my eyes fell on her, the girl.

I had seen her before with a blank look on her face but the look today was completely shocking; She was visibly not in control of her senses and was totally phased out. She wasn't aware of what was happening to her. Vandana was looking at her too. In spite of the noise, when Vandana moved her lips, I knew what was coming out of her mouth.

Methamphetamine.

* * *

I went and stood in front of Navya. Her eyes fell on me but her expression didn't change. Her eyes were watching me but her head didn't have the capacity to process me. And then she looked away, as if I was just another face she saw in a day.

Just then, DJ Vyk, who had been sitting beside her, got up. I didn't realize I had been staring at her rather awkwardly.

'What are you staring at?' he said, clearly wanting to pick a fight.

I couldn't get my eyes off Navya. There were a few more guys in the room and DJ Vyk seemed to hate us already. But I was too overwhelmed on seeing Navya to comprehend the tense environment building up in the room. Thankfully, Vandana was well in her senses.

She pulled me by my T-shirt out of that room.

We came out of Urban Pind. Out of the claustrophobia, when the air outside hit me, I actually been slapped by that guy. What was I doing? I was the guy who went to college every day, did his assignments on time, and talked to his mom everyday on the phone. And now, I was fighting guys at a club, travelling across city, chasing

99

a girl who couldn't think beyond some weird drug called Heroin. I am not that guy. Or am I?

We reached our flat, without exchanging a word during the whole return journey. This time, the normally chirpy Vandana seemed as tired and beaten as I did.

As she began to retire to her own room, I decided to ask what was killing me for curiosity and I called out to her, 'Vandana?'

'Yes?'

'Who was Divya?'

'Oh, she is nobody important; just somebody who was in love with me.'

* * *

The morning was a sombre one. Both of us were quiet. Suddenly, she was now a subdued, mellowed mature person that her age would have forced her to be. I didn't like her this way. I liked her jumping around, cracking annoying jokes and being a prick.

'I think I should go back to the Ashram,' Vandana said, as she sipped her tea sitting in the balcony of my flat.

'You think I would let you go?'

'My work here is done. I need to meditate and get my focus back.'

'The best way to get your focus back is to distract yourself. Get so busy that you have no time to worry about your focus.'

'I don't belong here. I belong to The Ashram. I have no work here.'

'Yes, you do. You are the one who would tell me how to chat up a drug-head.'

Vandana thought about it for a second. Divya, it seems, had broken her spirits. There was such a striking change in her from last night. She chewed on what I had just said, and then I saw a faint smile break on her face.

'I could be around for a few days,' she said.

I extended a hand. But Vandana was not impressed.

'Things are different now. Until yesterday, we were battling your past. But yesterday, we opened the Pandora box of my past too.'

'People who run away from circumstances are cowards. You are a strong believer of this school of thought, Vandana.'

She didn't have a reply to that. I had cornered her this time.

She nodded her head, indicating she would stay on, reluctantly though. This was it. We were in this together, once again.

'So where do we start?' I asked.

'I think I know where to start.'

'Where?'

'Aradhya,' she replied.

* * *

We were on our way to the publisher's office the next afternoon, when my phone started vibrating.

'Hiiiiii', Saloni gleamed as I picked the call. 'Wassup guruji? How is yoga treating you?'

'It's going alright. I am learning new things. Feeling a lot better about myself actually,' I said, realizing I really was feeling busy and better.

'Great. And here I am, having the time of my life in

South Africa.' Saloni was on a holiday with her husband.

'Wow. What all are you doing there?'

'Well, deep sea diving, walks on the beach, getting naughty on the jetty, I think we've done it all. Boy, this trip is so awesome!' I could feel her excitement and if I wasn't so preoccupied with my own stuff, I would have wanted to speak to her much longer.

'When are you back?'

'Well I am taking off on the evening of first of July. But I don't think I will be able to come at all. I want to live here.'

I wished her the very best and told her how happy I was for her. But I couldn't talk long. I was on my way to the publisher's office.

Aradhya, the receptionist, was where she was the last time. If she had come to know that we fooled her, it would jeopardize everything for us.

The moment her eyes laid on us, we had the answer to that question. She had come to know that we had been lying.

'You two!' she picked up the phone in front of her. 'Let me call the security to drag you imposters out.'

Vandana took a step forward and disconnected the call Aradhya was making.

'Come on, Aradhya *beta*, it wasn't *that* confidential an information,' Vandana said. I knew using words like *beta* didn't come to her naturally, but the situation demanded that.

'Are you serious? You made me give you the number of Mr Jaaved Khan and you think it's not that important information? You are from a competitor publishing house, aren't you? If you guys made one annoying call and he came to know that I gave you his number, he will have me fired in two minutes!'

'Jaaved Khan's number? You think we were after Jaaved Khan's number? We threw the paper away on which we wrote his number even before we got into the cab.'

'You think I will believe you after what you did?' Aradhya said.

'I know it's hard for you to believe us *beta*. But look at me. I'm almost your mother's age. Just come with me for a coffee and you will understand everything.' The mother's-age argument was actually a very strong one. And I bet curiosity must be eating up Aradhya too. So after some more convincing from both of us, Aradhya agreed for coffee during the lunch hour.

We agreed to meet at Costa Coffee outside the publisher's office. Vandana and I went there and waited for her.

'Vandana?'

'Samar?'

'Why do we keep finding ourselves waiting for people these days?'

'That's because you are on summer vacation and my life is a vacation any way. And people on vacation are mostly the people waiting.'

Aradhya walked in at one fifteen, as she had promised. And hence began the longest narration Aradhya would ever have to sit through. Vandana told her everything about me that she knew and how I had met her and why we were pursuing Navya. And we didn't even know if Aradhya had any information which could lead us to Navya or not.

And once Vandana was done telling the story, both of us looked at her without blinking our eyes, waiting to hear what comes out next from her mouth.

'Well,' Aradhya uttered and stopped midway. We knew that very moment that she did have an idea in her head but wasn't sure if she wanted to share.

'Well, there is this party happening. It's Ronnie's birthday party,' she finally said.

'Tell us more?' Vandana egged her on.

'I know Navya will come to that party because she is good friends with Ronnie. Ronnie is a TV actor but he meets all sorts of people. So there will be some people from Bollywood too. And it will be hard to get in. Ronny is in the process of penning a book and he thinks I can help him because I work at a publishing company. That explains my invitation, but luckily he doesn't know that I'm just a receptionist.'

'And what do you think will be happening at the party?' Vandana asked.

'Well, there are two parts of all such parties. One part is for the kids. There will be music and alcohol and there will be lots of models throwing themselves around to producers and directors and people who claim to be powerful. But the real party happens on the terrace. The first time you go there, you think it's a pathetic sight. Everyone is high on his favourite drugs. All they care about is where their next drag is coming from.'

Vandana nodded as I looked on. Urban Pind was one thing but gate crashing this party seemed a bit too much.

'Can you chalk out an idea which will take us inside?' I asked, almost without hope.

Aradhya gave a blank look. I could almost hear the Brownian whirring of thoughts inside Vandana's brain. She knew she had to come up with something fast as Aradhya would leave any moment.

'What sort of new people come to such a party?'

'Well, anybody who is friends with Ronnie. Or, famous people. And some drug dealers too, making sure people don't run out of anything. And the party is just ten days away which doesn't leave you with any time to be any of the above.'

'Friendship and fancy fame are ruled out,' I said.

'I guess that leaves us only one option,' Vandana said.

'Are you saying you're going to sell drugs at the party?' Aradhya asked.

'Worth a shot?' Vandana said with a not-so-confident smug smile.

'It's no joke being a dealer at these parties because they have good sources already. And I don't even know who to talk to if you want to deal in this party.'

'You have Ronnie's phone number?' I asked.

'Well, er. Yes. But I am not calling him.'

'Give his number to me,' Vandana said. Aradhya closed her eyes for two seconds, release some air from her mouth and then nervously gave her the number. She then left the table, without offering to pay the bill.

We came out, and without thinking much, Vandana dialled the number.

'Don't you want to plan something before calling him,' I asked her.

'Planning makes me nervous,' she said, as she waited for someone to pick the phone.

'Hello?' she heard a voice.

'Is it Ronnie?' she said, in a crisp accent.

'Yes? Who's this?'

'Hi Ronnie. This is Vandana here. I got to know about the party you're organizing on the 27th of June and I am told that you need some stuff for that.'

'What sort of stuff do you have?'

'The best. You won't find any equivalents around.'

'I mean what is it? Weed, Heroin, Meth? What the fuck do you have?'

'What do you want? We have everything.'

'Listen smart ass. We have enough of our dealers of our own and I don't even pick calls from new dealers unless someone I know has introduce me to them. But we don't have Meth for this particular party. So if you have Meth, come with five bags. Otherwise don't show your face.'

'I have the finest Meth you can find in Delhi. How do I get in?'

'Reach the venue and give me a call. And if the Meth is no good, don't think I won't break your head right there,' he said and hung up.

A part of Vandana was really petrified. This guy could make people pee in their pants just by his voice. Vandana wondered what will happen if he comes in front of her and shouts at her.

* * *

Meth is short for Methamphetamine and this drug is also known as Speed, Meth, chalk, ice, crystal, glass, mostly because it looks like ice or a white block.

Meth is one of the most dangerous drugs known today

and is extremely addictive. Although it can be taken orally or by snorting through the nose or injecting with a syringe, but the most popular method is to heat and smoke it.

It is known to stimulate the central nervous system and de-addiction is a rather challenging process.

Users will seek and use more Methamphetamine in order to get back to that state of pleasure, or to just feel 'normal' again, which results in a physical dependence on the drug. It is a never-ending cycle.

A person addicted to Meth experiences irritability, depression and other withdrawal symptoms and hence, de-addiction needs expert supervision.

People withdrawing from Methamphetamine can alternate from wanting to sleep all the time, to not being able to sleep. Withdrawal symptoms can last for several weeks.

One of the effects of Meth is prolonged wakefulness. Users don't sleep for days together and in extreme cases, can even lead to death.

This is what Wikipedia says about Meth.

The Time Has Come

The next morning, I woke up thinking of Navya. Until now, looking for her had been a personal motive. I was looking for her because I wanted myself to be at peace. For me, it was a search for closure. I needed to know where she was, and whether she was still in love with me. If she was, then we may or may not get back. But if she was not, I needed to know that too so that I could move on with life. It was a search for the rearmost catharsis.

But now, after having seen her in that condition, things had changed completely. I imagined the way she used to look in Goa: so unkempt and yet as vivacious as a fresh monsoon flower. And the same person now looked like a downtrodden rag picker. I apprehended any connection with her current condition because of my coldness towards her in Goa.

I called every friend of mine who had ever mentioned any drug in front of me. But none of them had any idea how to source Meth in Delhi; apparently, it was too hard a drug for them.

I searched on the net, I read how Meth was a big nuisance in the US, among other countries. The government had been trying to curb the use of this drug for years but wasn't able to do much. The challenge that the government faced was that Meth could be manufactured using simple Chemistry Lab instruments and by using ingredients which could be arranged from a simple Walmart store.

But it was also a process which required a lot of skill, and there was considerable risk. Therefore, the prices were high. There was more money to be had than anywhere else if a person masters the technique and proportions.

And then, it struck me. We would have to cook Meth ourselves. And without weighing the oddities, I plunged into how-to-cook-Meth. And I realized it was not impossible; It would be an uphill task but not impossible for sure. With much excitement I went and told this to Vandana.

It was the first of July. I was half way into my summer vacation. In a month's time, there would be companies coming to my campus for interviews. I was running out of time. We had nine days until the party. If we wanted to pull this off, we had to act fast.

'And on seeing us they'd be convinced that we are Meth dealers, right?' Vandana mocked at me when I told her my idea.

I smiled with confidence.

'You mean you are going to grow Meth in your backyard?' she said.

'Meth is not grown on plants. It's prepared in a Chemistry Lab. And you might remember that I am a Chemical Engineer in the making.'

'Dude, we are talking real complex drugs here! You are a kid. If it was this easy then wouldn't every one start cooking it? Somehow I can't convince myself,' she said.

'I will have to work sleeplessly just to put the theory together,' I said.

'And how are you planning to put all this theory together?'

'Well, this is where Uncle Fester comes in.'

'Uncle who?' Vandana reacted.

'Uncle Fester. His real name was Steve Priesler and he was from the US from the early 1980s. Basically, he was a nut head, famous for producing explosives and blowing things up in the Chemistry Lab when he was in school. He was an Industrial Chemist, who, after getting arrested for possession of Methamphetamine was sentenced to probation. Outraged, Fester borrowed a typewriter from a fellow inmate in jail, and began writing his first book.'

'What does that have to with us?' Vandana asked.

'The name of his book was 'Secrets of Methamphetamine Manufacture'. He has listed six different ways of Meth manufacture for a beginner, which is exactly what we need.'

'I am not sure. So we walk into a bookstore and ask for that book?'

'You can't. Such a book can never get published in India,' I said.

'Yep.'

'And then we would have to get all the raw material and I have no idea how we are going to do that.

'And you are going to do all this in nine days?'

'Well, er, yes, with a bit of luck, yes.'

'It's an extremely steep task, even if you were Einstein,' Vandana said, dismissing me.

'Do you have a better idea?' I asked her. She had to shut up.

'Samar listen, you are actually going to cook one of the most dangerous drugs in the world. I mean, if we manufacture it and give it to Ronnie, it will be actually smoked by someone. Are you okay with being the reason behind someone spoiling his life using the drugs made with your hands?'

'I had thought of that. But then, it is Navya's rest of life which was at stake. I would never be able to forgive myself for being the one to cook Meth. But this is one trade off I was willing to make. Those Meth-heads were anyway going to get it from one source or another. But I am only thinking of Navya right now. That's one innocent life that we can save.'

Thankfully, Vandana nodded on hearing my argument. This was important for me because I did not want to drag her into it without her unfettered conviction. And I was seeking validation from her. I wanted her to have resonance with my thoughts.

'So how do you think we will get this book?' she asked.

'Well, one of my friends, Saloni is in South Africa right now. She is taking off this evening and will land early morning tomorrow. I had identified an online book store there which would deliver the book the same day, if Saloni was willing to play along.'

I told Saloni to pick a packet which would get delivered to her room in the hotel. She didn't argue and instead, joked about what will happen if she gets caught by the customs.

She didn't realize but it was a genuine concern. But I was also confident that Saloni and her husband wouldn't look suspicious to the custom authorities and were unlikely to be stopped.

* * *

We went to receive Saloni at the airport and I took the packet from her as soon as I could. I didn't open it in front of her even though she showered a thousand questions at me. Thankfully, Vandana and Saloni hit off instantly. Vandana had enough stories from The Ashram to keep her amused. And we dropped Saloni and her husband to their house safe and sound.

I jumped into the book 'Secrets of Methamphetamine Manufacture' the moment we reached the flat. The book opened with a long list of disclaimers and precautions.

I started reading from the first line on the first page and stopped only at the last line of the last page around forty hours later. Every waking minute, I could feel the clock ticking. The read was mentally sapping but I wanted to make sure I knew everything there was to know about the process.

I had my notebook in front of me all this while in which I strategized as to how would I go about doing the whole thing. And the moment I was done reading the book, I sat in front of my laptop and starting Googling; with watery eyes and droopy eyelids. Looking at the computer screen, I didn't realize when I fell asleep. And then I woke up, brushed my teeth, went to the toilet and got back to reading on the net again.

In the next eight hours, I had read everything written about cooking Meth on Google, researching on every ingredient, where we could get it, and for how much.

Phew. Information overload; I needed to calm myself down. I needed to organize the information. I needed to plan and prioritize. I had to think of an action plan. I had to refresh my skills in the Chemistry Lab.

* * *

It was at ten in the night that I felt I was ready and we could start with the actual work from the next morning. I was sitting in my room and I felt like sharing the news with Vandana. I walked into her room. I forgot to knock because of the excitement.

What I saw was a shocker. Vandana was lying on her bed, staring at nothing, with tears rolling down her eyes.

I didn't know how to react for a second.

'I was making tea for myself. You need one too?' I awkwardly asked her.

She nodded. And when tea was ready, I called her to the balcony to have it.

I couldn't beat around the bush.

'Vandana, you remember how you once said that you will tell me your story when the time comes?'

'Yes. I do.'

'I think the time has come.'

Vandana Speaks

Vandana was always a bright child. She was born and brought up on the streets of Patiala and had typical features of Punjab embedded in every cell of her body. She was a family star because of the poems she could recite at four and the track and field events she could win at the age of twelve. Everybody could gauge that she was way ahead of her peer group. Even though it amused everyone, it worried Vandana's mom as she thought that it would be difficult to get suitors to marry her sharp and cut-above-the-rest girl.

There was no culture of studies for girls beyond twelfth standard in her family. This legacy was so deeply internalized by Vandana that she didn't even realize that she should study further.

But she was lucky that she was spotted by Divya ma'am. Divya had an eye for sharp brains and gregarious chatty extroverts. The two started talking, and Divya managed to successfully dazzle her with the beauty of the city of New Delhi. Vandana wanted to take the next bus to Delhi.

Hell broke loose in the Manchanda household that day. But Vandana's father was a progressive fellow and he let his daughter go, even though he knew they would never be able to relate to their daughter again if she went to

Delhi. She would adapt to Delhi like a bird does to the sky and become an alien to Patiala.

Divya had an Interior Designing firm in South Delhi and Vandana began as an office help: making tea for the employees, dusting before they came in, and delivering papers and getting print outs. On the first day, she was darn scared of a computer. She thought it was a state of the art machine, which can fall apart by one wrong touch and can completely crash by the press of a wrong key.

But slowly and gradually, she started noticing the patterns in the way people worked on the computer. She started realizing that the people working on those machines were not exceptionally sharper than her. And then she decided to sit down in front of the computer and just experiment until things started making sense.

Divya loved her for her sincerity. Vandana was not outstandingly pretty but she was definitely presentable. And she had the knack of learning things much faster than other people. Divya asked her to move in with her, and leave behind the small room that Vandana had rented. They started living together and Vandana took on the task of cooking for her too.

Soon, Vandana learnt as much as a regular draftsman in Divya's office. Her salary rose too, and also the respect she got from people in the office. She was naturally likeable and it worked for her. She had gotten used to the city. She felt no urge to go back to Patiala, as the rustic ways of that city would now seem foreign to her. Delhi was her new pace and home. Weeks passed into months and further into years.

Divya was unmarried and almost reaching thirty then. She was a chain smoker. She fitted every stereotype of a spoilt brat and the fact that her firm was doing well she had a lot of time on her hands to stay spoilt.

But Vandana began to notice things she couldn't understand. Even though Divya lived alone, she never got male guests. Instead, she spent disproportionate amounts of time in her bedroom with some of her female friends. Divya had short hair, lean body and wore heaps of *kajal* in her eyes every single day. The more Vandana noticed Divya, the surer she became that Divya actually liked girls, instead of boys, even though there was no single reason which she could pin point.

The suspense ended when Vandana spotted Divya kissing one of her female friends in the living room. Divya had forgotten than Vandana was around and huge part of her was relieved that finally Vandana knew that Divya was a lesbian. Divya had cultivated a liking for Vandana in those months.

So the next night that Divya drank, she offered vodka to Vandana too. Vandana would have said no if she knew how to say no to Divya. That only egged on Divya, making her believe that Vandana will succumb to anything.

But when Divya made her real advances, Vandana backed out. She told her that even though she respected and loved Divya in her own way, she couldn't bring herself to do it, no matter what.

Divya backed out on that night but Vandana became a continuous tease for her. She would shop for her and encourage her to wear dresses and flaunt her body. It turned her on, and she derived a weird pleasure from having a tease in front of her eyes all day long.

It had started off as Vandana being an office help. But they were now more like two friends living together, one of which didn't do any domestic chore. Eventually, Vandana joined a Diploma course in Interior Designing. It was a two year course and Divya didn't have any qualms about sponsoring the fee. And the next thing she knew, Vandana was more capable than her employees who had three year degrees on their CVs.

It was Vandana's twenty third birthday. She told Vandana she had to come out with her for dinner as they just had to celebrate her birthday in style. Divya called up Vandana and asked her to come downstairs in the parking where she was waiting.

When Vandana reached downstairs, she was blown away by what she saw. Divya was standing in front of her car wearing a black tuxedo, like a gentleman. She had a pencil moustache probably made with her *kajal* and she was wearing a hat, covering her hair.

Divya did look like a gentleman.

'You had a problem with my gender. Well today, I am a guy,' Divya said in a husky voice.

Vandana had no idea how to react. But she was overwhelmed with the effort put by Divya. Divya escorted Vandana to her seat in the car, and together they drove to a fine dine restaurant.

When they reached back home, both of them were slightly more than tipsy. And both of them knew what was to follow.

Divya closed the door behind her, as both of them entered the flat. Every line Divya spoke in her husky tone, Vandana got a little turned on.

Vandana had never slept with anyone before. And at twenty three, her hormones had begun to play with her mind. She needed to experience what a physical touch was like. And Divya was the only one with whom she was comfortable enough. So when Divya put in so much effort, Vandana's decided to give in that night.

Their heads moved forward. For the first time in Vandana's life, she was going to kiss a person, even though this was not how she had imagined her first kiss to be.

But after a few seconds, Vandana was overcome with a sinking feeling. She wasn't supposed to like this.

'We should stop,' she said, gently, pushing Divya away.

'It's too late to stop,' Divya said, and held Vandana's head with her hands and kissed her again.

'But it's not right.'

Divya wanted to give up. She didn't want to force herself; but lust overcame the better of her. She couldn't stop herself.

Vandana was enjoying it physically but her mind was not ready for it. Her breasts wanted Divya to feel them, her erect nipples and the lumps in her throat vouched for it. Divya's tongue on the tender veins on the tilted neck of Vandana made her stomach stir with pleasure. And to top it all, Divya's words and heavy sighs were driving her crazy.

Vandana reciprocated and they plunged into it.

It was smooth at first. Divya was giving her space enough to get comfortable with their nakedness. She explored Vandana's levelled body. She gripped her fleshy love handles which made Vandana a little conscious. She whispered praises about Vandana's curves in her ears as she roved around. Vandana let her take charge.

And then Divya unlocked the drawer in which she stacked her toys. Vandana felt the ecstasy of those powerful vibrators rubbing between her thighs. She found herself involuntarily moving her hips. Divya then licked Vandana's fingers and guided them inside her body. The moans kindled Vandana to pleasure her partner more.

Vandana experienced the sweetness of sweat, the thrill of her lost inhibitions and wonder of an orgasm for the first time.

* * *

When Divya had slept off, Vandana started doing exactly what she shouldn't have done. She got introspective.

She realized she needed a direction in life. She sat in silence and was enveloped by negative thoughts. She thought of her parents and what they expected of her. The little conversation she had with them had gotten increasingly strained ever since she got used to Delhi. They wanted her to get married, that too in Patiala, even though her Dad knew this was unlikely. And here she was now, having bared herself in front of another woman because of lust.

She thought how her father would react if he came to know. Honour killing wasn't impossible. And disowning was an absolute surety.

She decided to try sleeping, instead of pinning her sexual orientation. While she was going to bed, she knew that whatever just happened was not one of those instances that they would laugh over a few years down the line. She could not go back to Patiala and she did not actually need a man either.

Vandana did not expect Divya to enter their room with morning coffee but she did expect some warmth and intimacy after the last night.

Divya had already taken a shower and was getting ready to go somewhere. Vandana, sitting up on the bed, asked her about her schedule for the day. Divya, while applying her deep red nail paint, replied, 'I'm going to see Tanya.' Vandana knew about Tanya from her frequent visits and long stays in Divya's room. And Divya, left the house, only to come back late after midnight. Divya, who had waited for her almost the entire day, could instantly smell cigarette from her clothes and alcohol from her breath. She put the semi-conscious Divya to bed. Vandana knew the wayward woman Divya was. She's never been in a committed relationship before and her partners changed frequently too. And yet, she wanted to sit down and have a serious conversation about her fidelity.

Next morning Divya woke Vandana up to get her some lime water, which was to tone down her hangover. Vandana tried talking to her, but she thought she'd hear out first. Divya started hurling abuses at Tanya. She had left Divya for someone else. Vandana kept mum. Hiding her own pain and agony, she tried calming Divya down.

Life went by without Vandana realizing a thing. After a point, her family gave up on her. She stopped getting invites of her cousin's weddings and her annual summer visit was discontinued in her twenty seventh birthday. Divya made love to her only when she was shit drunk and alone at home. But this was enough sexual gratification for Vandana. She made peace with it. She couldn't imagine doing anything with anyone else.

Vandana fell for the terrible want which slowly became a need. Now that she had Divya once, she wanted her again. She was suddenly more dependent than Divya was. And it's only human nature to want what you can't have.

Divya's partners never stopped flowing in. Vandana's body was more or less objectified to Divya as per her needs. She took Vandana for granted. She knew that whatever she does, she always had Vandana waiting for her at home. Vandana tolerated everything till the time she could. She knew Divya loved her and was dependent on her but she was too free spirited to be committed to one person for life.

Years went by, until Divya reached her early fifties. The Interior Designing firm now had a good team of twenty. And Vandana hadn't visited the office for a decade. She was in her late thirties herself. Most people knew they were a couple. And that Divya wasn't really the faithful types.

Over the last two years, Vandana had picked up a chronic cough, which she thought was due to allergy or some local recurring infection. But weeks passed and medicines couldn't heal it. She started spending sleepless nights due to shortness of breath and shooting pain in the chest, sometimes extending to her shoulders. She had also passed out four times within seven weeks. Worst of all, Divya didn't notice any of it. She would casually inquire her but not notice the consistency of Vandana's falling health graph.

Vandana knew enough to know that she couldn't take it lightly now. Both, her illness and Divya's callousness towards her. But this was life as she knew it. It's not easy to break inertia of almost twenty years. But she would have to do it. She had some money with her. And Divya came back home that evening, Vandana was not there. She had moved out.

After a few rejections, she got herself a job at another interior designing firm. She rented herself a flat and paid her first visit to the doctor after settling down. Vandana also changed her number; so Divya could have had no way of locating her.

After she discussed her symptoms with the doctor, she was immediately ordered to undergo various examinations. Thankfully, she had enough cash to pay for the tests.

The MRI made her feel claustrophobic. The X-rays made her feel sick. The various blood tests were actually a respite because they didn't pain as much as she had expected. And when she was done with all the tests, she waited to see the look on the doctor's face when he saw the reports.

She craved for someone to hold onto. Somebody whom she could hold tight and express how scared she was, maybe shed a tear or two. A part of her thought that maybe there was something wrong with her: She couldn't keep up with her parents. And then she couldn't hold Divya's attention too. Did she deserve to die alone? And die of a disease she couldn't have thought would ever happen to her.

It was *lung cancer*.

* * *

On her way back home, Vandana prayed that no one ever had to sit through being told that she had lung cancer. But more than that, she prayed that no one would have sit through being told that she had lung cancer *alone*. No one should have no-one to call to share the sorrow with. No one should feel the way she was feeling at that moment.

She went home. She had told the doctor that she would be back the next day, better mentally prepared. The doctor agreed to wait, as the cancer hadn't spread too much. Not *as yet*.

The next day, the doctor laid out the situation in front of her. Her cancer hadn't spread too much. But the treatment was expensive. But he also laid out the options of getting funding for her treatment. But Vandana went on her tangent inside her head.

What she heard was, *'You can either ask Divya or your parents for help. Or you can die peacefully, alone.'*

She knew that she was perhaps not in the best of frame of minds to make a decision. She had already lost her self-respect in front Divya and did not want to go back to her. She had insulted Vandana enough and taken away her cheer from her; she would not beg in front of her now. Her parents had been out of the picture for way too long. The last thing she wanted to tell her seventy year old parents was that she was dying and needed her help after having ignored them for two decades.

And then she thought who was she living for? Or rather, who would miss her if she was gone? She had broken every relationship that had come her way.

With these thoughts in mind, she decided that the expensive treatment was not for her. And decided to spend her final few days doing something she wanted to do in her final few days. Meditate. And be happy.

*   *   *

That's how, with a cancer struck body, Vandana landed at the Ashram. She needed strength to accept her end. And nobody else could give it to her. It had to come from within. And the only way she knew she could get that was through meditation.

It was May when she had landed there. And the moment she stepped in the Ashram, she knew she wanted to spend the rest of her life (whatever remained of it) in this place.

She had initially applied for a one month's stay. But when the month ended, she realized she had nowhere to go. Where would she be, if not here? And also, that she was now in love with The Ashram. She liked the non-judging nature of the people. Nobody cared about your past. Future worries were almost non-existent for these people. All everyone was interested in was the present. So when her one month in the Ashram ended, she spoke to people and extended her stay.

She lived on pain killers she had bought off the shelf from the chemist. She blanked out once or twice but nothing to alarm people around her and she managed to keep her cancer to herself. She used to wonder what was happening in the other world. She hadn't contacted her parents in years now. In leaps and bounds, she managed to ignore her disease, to forget Divya and lead a normal life.

She became a new person. Her loneliness made her goofy and happy-go-lucky. She didn't have a family. Even though she loved everyone at the Ashram, there was no one in particular who she could call a friend. But this changed the moment she laid her eyes on Samar. She noticed the restlessness in his eyes and she wanted to know the reason behind it. And for the first time in her life, she felt motherly love towards someone, which she felt she was incapable of. She wanted to be friends with him, know him better and if she could, help him get rid of the negativity in his life.

Like A Foot Soldier In A Battle

Vandana and I were sitting in my balcony, staring at the traffic passing by as she told me her story. In that hour, as she recounted everything she had been through, her complete persona changed in my eyes. She had been a goofy, carefree person till now. And suddenly, she seemed more mature than anyone I ever knew.

I could have had Goosebumps but I didn't check. I didn't check because way too many things were running through my head. If ever someone's view could change in my eyes in a matter of minutes, it was today.

Who could have said that this lively ball of energy was facing death, straight in the eye? And she ignored it like it was an insignificant corn in her foot.

I thought about myself. What was the biggest worry I had ever had? When had I been the most scared in life? What was the worst that had ever happened to me?

There were people living with bigger pains, and if they could live them with such élan, why couldn't I? I suddenly rewinded my thoughts when I thought that all her coughing was sheer dramatics. My head hung in shame.

And once I had absorbed the shock, I began to come back to my senses. And my thoughts got a bit more rational.

'So how much money are we talking about?' I asked her.

'I don't know. Probably around a half a crore or something,' she said in her characteristic nonchalant way.

I made a little promise to myself. I felt like a foot soldier who is part of a huge battle. The way he looks at the force in front of him and he makes a little promise to his motherland, that no matter what happens to him, he will make sure I protect you with all it might. I made a similar promise to myself, that I will try to save her by everything that I can do. I wasn't sure how much I could do. To save up half a crore would probably take more than half my life. And Vandana didn't have all day to start the treatment.

My first idea was maybe requesting Vandana into talking to Divya. But then, there must have been a good reason why Vandana had not spoken to her. The little that I had seen of her, I had my doubts about how he would react.

I thought of talking to mom, but I knew that half a crore was a huge sum even for her. She would believe some lady was duping me into paying the money or something.

I looked at Vandana, looking out of the balcony, as if she was on a weekend break from a corporate job. When she had seen me for the first time, she noticed the unrest in my life on my face. And here I was, having spent more than a month with her, without a hint of the colossal physical and mental pain she was handling.

* * *

Standing in the balcony, Vandana had my wallet in her hand, as she had told me her story. She had been fiddling with it for quite some time, without doing anything with it. If nothing else, her action diffused the tension in the air.

'What are you looking for?' I finally asked her.

'Guys your age are supposed to carry condoms in their wallets. But I don't think you're that interesting.'

'Then what you looking for?'

'Maybe I'm looking for your debit card,' she said.

And she finally opened my wallet and looked around. What caught her eye was something small, dark and spherical.

'What on earth is this?'

'It's a coffee bean,' I replied, as a thousand memories of that coffee bean came back to my mind. Although I had felt it many times in my wallet, I had gotten so used to seeing it there that my mind didn't register it.

'Are you keeping it there so that you can have coffee when you're stuck in the middle of nowhere?'

'It's a long story.'

'I love long stories.'

'It was a nice and breezy evening in Goa. Navya was wearing a yellow dress, which flew around just enough to keep me interested and not embarrass her. There were days when I could sense that it was taking Navya all her energy to stop herself from wrapping her arms around me. I called them non-verbal cues. Her body language shouted that she wanted me. Navya wanted to say something to me, but instead, she stopped at a coffee shop on the beach, went up to the counter and got one single coffee bean. This was that bean.

She gave it to me and asked me, 'Do you know The Coffee Bean Theory?'

'No,' I said.

'If someone gives you a coffee bean, you should keep it with you. And as you take it, you can make a wish. And the wish will come true if you keep the bean with you. Once the wish comes true, you need to pass on the bean to somebody.'

'You mean it's like a good luck charm?'

'Yes. Kind of.'

'Hmm. Did your wish come true?' Vandana asked

I didn't reply. I remembered clearly what I had wished for. In fact, I didn't even know whether the wish came true or not. Navya was in love with me at that time, which I couldn't reciprocate. And she was such a sweet and adorable girl that I actually wished that Navya would stop loving me such that she doesn't get hurt. I really hoped that it hadn't come true, at this point. I needed her, with me.

'Don't make that face now,' Vandana broke my chain of thought.

'Okay, then tell me, what are we doing next?'

* * *

By now, I was PhD in Meth Cooking. I felt I knew everything there was to know.

There were tens of processes. I could use phenol acetone in a tube furnace and then use reductive emanation to yield Methamphetamine. But then, I had searched all night for a way to get our hands on Methylamine, an important ingredient in the process. There were a few other processes and each had one or the other major road block.

The process I finally narrowed down on was simpler than the others and most ingredients and materials seemed quite accessible. But there was just one ingredient which was hard to acquire.

Pseudoephedrine, more commonly called 'pseudo'. Psuedo is a highly controlled substance. But it is a fairly common ingredient in common cold and anti-allergic medicines. But to extract it from those medicines is another task.

Nevertheless, I slept off with the thought of narrating the strategy to Vandana on the next day, with six days to go for the party. With no TV in the house, she was beginning to lose her cool, with nothing to do all day. But then, I hoped to make her wait worth the while when I would tell her the plan.

* * *

'So, you're saying we sneak into the Chemistry Lab of your college and cook Meth there?' Vandana said, with the most surprised expression I had seen on her.

'Yes. That's exactly what I'm saying.'

'So you're saying, that a simple little Chemistry Lab of your college has all the equipment for cooking a drug like Methamphetamine?'

'Yes, almost everything. Remaining things we can get at any chemical store.'

'You mean, like *everything*?'

'Yes, everything, except the most important ingredient – pseudo.'

'And how do you plan on getting that?'

'Well, I have a plan for that.'

'Mind telling?'

'Well, have you ever wondered that why is the room you live in so well furnished?'

'Because somebody used to live there. Your ex-roommate perhaps.'

'Yeah. His name is Roy. He used to be my best friend. He was the one who was giving mouth to mouth to Kanika when I thought was kissing her.'

'Where's he now?'

'He is presently interning at Tanroxy Pharmaceuticals in Manesar. You know Manesar?'

'No.'

'Manesar is around two hour drive from Delhi. It's famous for great resorts and some factories in the area. Tanroxy is a prominent factory in the area. They had come to our college to look for an intern and picked Roy.'

'But why are you telling me all this?'

'I am telling you all this, because Tanroxy is a major manufacturer of Pseudoephedrine in India.'

'It's like God wants us to succeed in this crazy mission,' Vandana gave a broad smile.

'Yeah. He has been showing us the way at every point. I realized that way before. I don't know about you, but that was very important for me.'

'Was it? Why?'

'Because we are cooking Meth, Vandana. It's not the most ethical thing to do. And knowing that God is with us is important. It means he thinks we are not doing something wrong. We are doing something unethical to save Navya's life. And what can be better than knowing that even God think that's okay.'

Vandana understood my point. She was impressed with the plan I had built up. She could finally appreciate my three days' effort.

'You've really thought this through.'

'That's how I do things.'

'So what is the next step?'

'The next step is that you go to a chemical store and buy these chemicals,' I said, as I handed over the list to Vandana.

She took the list. And squinted her eyes on what seemed very foreign words to her.

'Phosphus? I can't even pronounce these words. Why should I go to the market? You'd have to do this.'

'Because these are suspicious chemicals. And you wouldn't look suspicious buying them. If I buy them, people ask questions because I look like a guy up to some mischief. If you wear a suit and go and ask for them, you will look like a high school chemistry lab assistant or something.'

Vandana bought that argument, while the real reason was that I was just plain lazy. I needed time alone in this house after the three day mental acrobat. Perhaps, a TV in the living room would have been handy at this time. I liked having Vandana around in the house, but still, it would be nice to have some time away from her at this stage.

Once she was gone, I sat in my balcony and made some tea for myself. I wasn't much of a tea person but it's relaxing to have herbal tea sometimes. I looked at the street in front of me and thought of the plan I had made. And I realized that somewhere in between reading that book, I was beginning to get obsessed. The sight of Navya, lying on the couch, in unconscious state spurred me on. I would go any distance to make this worth; losing sleep for nine days was the least of them.

The only unpleasant part was getting back in touch with Roy. As I said, even though officially we were on talking terms, things had been really awkward between us.

I wanted to make this call when Vandana was not home, and perhaps, now was a good time.

Roy was staying in the company campus itself. He must have been taken aback on seeing my name on his screen.

'Heeyyy Samar,' he said, in a lively voice, as if things had never been awkward between us. I think things were half sorted on that moment itself.

'Hi Roy. How are you? How's the internship going?'

And then he told me about his company, his project and a few more boring details. I asked him if he had girls in his company and he had a story or two to share. At least in that fleeting moment, it was as if things had never been wrong.

But it's one thing to talk normally on the phone. But it's quite another to help a friend getting his hand on restricted substances.

'Roy, actually, I called because I was planning to come to Manesar today.'

'Oh wow! What for? Something related to your summer project? You are coming alone or is there a team tagging along?'

'Well, I'll have a friend along. Her name is Vandana.'

'New girlfriend?'

'She is almost my mother's age,' I said.

'So what brings you to Manesar?'

'It's a long story Roy. And I need your help for two very important things. I have had a long summer and have some stories to tell you. Have some rum ready for the evening,' I said and hung up.

It was a heart-warming conversation with Roy after a long time. Maybe I had missed a friend who knew where I came from and what I thought. There is nothing like guy bonding.

Like A Mother
Protecting Her Child

The door opened a while later and Vandana entered, coughing. As much as she tried to shove away the topic of her illness, the fact that she was getting worse every passing day was a reality. She still wasn't in pain, but very soon, her body will start to visibly give away.

She came back to the living room, with her trademark smile, which I could understand was painfully forced. While she was showing me the jazzy bottles and other utilities she had brought, I realized I had to take care of her before I did anything else.

We had six days until Aradhya's party. I went back to my notebook and re-planned things to see if I could do those things in five days. I needed to devote a day to Vandana too.

So I messaged Roy, that we will come tomorrow instead of today. And went and sat down in front of my computer. I told myself until I would have found a way to collect money for Vandana's treatment. I was a great believer in the ability of the internet. Yes, Google has been added to the list of 33 million Gods we have in India.

I called up all the cancer NGOs I could find on the net.

But the amount was way beyond their capacity. I went and met one of the biggest NGOs, and they promised me a support of up to three lakhs, if I could make a credible doctor say that it will save her life. But it was far from enough.

I searched some more. And then I came across a story with the title, 'Sympathy Over Touching Viral Photo - Saves Dying Dog's Life.'

The story was about a man who's dog was dying of arthritis but he couldn't get it cured because he didn't have enough money for it. So he posted a touching photograph of himself with the dog on the internet and asked for donation. The photograph went viral because of its emotional connect and people donated in large numbers, resulting in saving the dog's life.

I got an idea when I read about this. And I decided to build a website of my own.

I registered the domain *savevandana.com* and set up everything in next four hours. I asked for donations on the site and promoted it everywhere I could. I shared the link on my Facebook profile, tweeted it and put it up on my dormant blog too. I messaged whoever I could and asked them to share it as well. And slowly, the website crossed a hundred, a thousand and then ten thousand clicks.

And I waited, staring at my bank account, for the money to come in. Small trickles began to flow in. But the big flourish didn't come all day. I realized I had done what I needed to do. From here onwards, I would have to let it build. And take care of it from the corner of my eye.

It was dark and late in the day. I checked the clock on the wall, it was three o'clock. We were leaving for

Manesar at around twelve the next day. Which meant I could have a much needed good long sleep, even though I had my doubts that whether I would be able to sleep or not, with so much happening in my head.

* * *

The drive to Manesar was a long one. With every passing minute, my bond with Vandana was getting stronger and stronger. Definitely, she was the closest person to me in the world at that moment. And to think that I didn't know her at all until so recently did not seem weird anymore. Length of time doesn't always decide the proximity you feel with someone.

Vandana was in a pensive mood herself, as we sat in the car. I had a feeling she would say something soon to diffuse the tension.

'Tell me more about her Samar,' Vandana said. She had said it to diffuse the tension in the air and lighten up a little bit. She had accomplished it completely.

'What do you want to hear?' I asked.

'I don't know. Something about another of your walks on the beach?'

'Hmm. So this one time, we were walking along the beach. We were not close to the shack that day and had come pretty far. We had a cone of ice cream each in our hands and it was melting at an unmanageable rate.'

'How do you eat this thing now?' I asked Navya

She looked at me. Hung her tongue out. And made a long lick starting from her wrist, where the ice cream had come down melting. After finishing the long smooth lick, 'that's how,' she said.

'Eeew, disgusting!' I grimaced.

'You're so not my type,' she replied.

'Thanks. I don't want to be your type. What does that mean anyway?'

'Well, I normally like guys, who, you know, are assertive.'

'And you think I'm not assertive?' I said. She laughed. 'In fact, anyone who spends more than a month in Goa has been assertive about something.'

'You're stubborn, Samar. It's different.'

'I prefer stubborn over assertive. A stubborn guy does things. An assertive guy pesters others to do things for him.'

'You're just amusing yourself.'

'Am I? So that's what you were looking for, huh? Assertiveness?'

'No.'

'Then?' I asked.

'I guess I was looking for you,' she replied. 'Just that I was hoping you would be looking for me too.'

* * *

At around four, we reached Manesar. We called Roy as we stood at the company entrance.

Roy came to the gate to see us and he was elated. The moment he laid his eyes on Vandana, he knew they would get along. Roy wasn't prepared for the fact that we will actually be staying with him in his room. Thankfully, it was okay for him and wasn't too risky in his company.

Roy had a spacious room and he was too chivalrous to let Vandana sleep on the floor. So Vandana got the bed, as Roy and I lay down on the floor.

And once our bags were shoved in the corner, introductions made, inhibitions and awkwardness dropped, alcohol bottles opened, it was time to start narrating the summer to him.

* * *

Roy went from shit drunk to absolutely sober in 0.1 second when I told him why exactly we were in Manesar.

'You guys are fucking crazy?' he said with a hint of slur. There was definite panic in his voice, as if we were going to push him and make him do it with us. I knew I could talk him into it. But the only challenge was that we had to do it tomorrow. We didn't have much time.

Ideally, I would have dismissed this conversation for the time being and touched the topic only next day. But Roy would have woken up the next morning and headed to work. It wouldn't have given me much of an opportunity.

'There are more than one lives at stake Roy. We will have to do this.'

'Yes, and one of those lives will be mine if I go ahead with this. You have lost your mind. I am really sorry but I would really appreciate it if you guys leave next morning.'

Ouch. That hurt. It hurt so much that if Navya's life was not on the line, I would have definitely left that moment itself, instead of waiting till the morning. But I was desperate. And I needed what I was asking for. So with all the power that I could muster, I laughed it off.

'It's not something you laugh about Samar.'

'Look at it this way Roy. What if you get caught? You are kicked out of this company internship? So what? Look at me, I am faking my internship any way. You can also fake your internship if you get kicked out, no?'

'Shut the fuck up now Samar!' Roy said, now seriously angry. 'Pseudoephedrine is a restricted substance. If we get caught with pseudo on us, we don't just get fired from our internship. We get fucking thrown into a jail with a non-bailable warrant. And that is not something I am up for!'

I could see that the argument was over there. There was no way Roy would help us on this when his reaction was like this. And with enough awkwardness in the room to break some glasses, we switched off the light, and made some futile attempts to fall asleep.

After a while, I noticed that Roy, who had slept right next to me, was not there. He was sitting on the table, with a piece of paper in front of him, as he scribbled fervently on it. I rubbed my eyes and got up on my feet. I went to the washroom and splashed some water on my face after brushing my teeth.

Vandana was still deep asleep. I went and sat in the chair in front of Roy. And threw a cursory glance at what he was scribbling.

As I leaned in, Roy looked at me in all seriousness, 'This is a rough sketch of this company campus,' he said. And then it struck me. Something had crossed his mind during the night and he had changed his mind. He was in!

'This is the main gate where you entered. And this, over here, is where we are sitting right now. The company campus has three major parts. First is the office area, where everybody sits. Second is the laboratory area, where all the tests and experiments take place. And the third, and the one we need to focus on, is the storage area where all chemicals, restricted and otherwise, are stored.'

'So here is the plan,' he continued. 'Every day, I take

a coffee break at three in the afternoon. Today, instead of having coffee, I will see you here, at this point exactly,' he said and marked a dot on the company layout. 'From here, we will move in this direction because fewer people hangout in this area. And then, bypassing the main reception, we will cross over to the restricted chemicals storage room, here.'

I was listening in all seriousness. Because of Roy's mischievous nature, people often forgot that he had a sharp mind. And I was reminded of it after several years.

'The government has laid out security measures which need to be taken while storing restricted chemicals. But I don't think any Indian company cares to follow those guidelines. Tanroxy normally employs some untrained guards and I have a feeling that section will be no different.'

'But still, we would need some sort of authorization to enter the restricted area, no?'

'Yes, we would. But we are lucky in that respect. In my internship, we are using a restricted substance too. So I will get written permission from my guide to let us to that part of the storage.'

Once again, the feeling that God is with us, and that he wants us to succeed at this crazy task took me over and I found new morale to do it. It was the sixth of July, with four days to go for the party. Time was slipping by. We would have to get our hands on Psuedo today itself and head back to Delhi the same evening.

Roy was leaving for work. But there was only one question hanging in my head. I had to ask him this.

'Roy?' I said.

'Yes?'

'But why? Why are you risking so much for us?'

Roy looked at me. Initially shocked, he then smiled. 'Brother, I have given you enough pain. I will consider this as a part of my redemption. But maybe, it will alleviate some pain I am feeling for whatever happened last year,' he said and closed the door behind him, as he left for work, leaving Vandana and me alone in his room.

'He is a good guy,' Vandana said as soon as he was out of earshot.

* * *

We looked around a bit through the afternoon. And by the time it was three, an instant adrenalin rush took over and we met Roy, exactly where we had decided to meet.

'Here, wear this,' he said, as he handed over a badge to me. I wore it around my neck.

'Who is Avinash Kumar?' I asked, reading the name on the badge.

'He is my project mate. With this badge on you, the guards will get even more casual about you.'

Definitely, he understood the seriousness of this now. And his attention to detail was phenomenal. He showed me an official looking piece of paper.

'What is this?' I asked.

'This is our ticket to enter any section of storage area,' he said. I supposed it meant it was the request letter for some restricted chemical.

We followed the root he had explained to me. And our first stoppage came when we crossed over to the storage area. Roy had planned for this. We showed the request letter for a chemical and our badges and they let us in. Now the next step was to look for pseudoephedrine. The chemicals were arranged alphabetically and thankfully, it didn't take us very long to locate the alphabet P.

I stopped close to the entrance of the section and let Roy go ahead, so that I can keep a check if someone was coming. As Roy went in, I looked around hoping no one would come. I kept one eye at the entrance, and the other in the direction where Roy had gone, hoping he would come soon.

But Roy didn't. Instead, a big moustached man appeared on the wrong side of me.

'Hey hi! Can I help you? What chemical you're looking for?'

'Not really. I am just looking for some Phosphorus. I'll just pick some and go.'

'Oh great. What lab are you from?'

Now this was tricky. I didn't know what lab Roy was from. What was worse was that I didn't know the names of any lab in this company.

'I am from Chemical Analysis,' I blurted the first name that came to my mind.

'Which scientist?'

'Dr Mehrotra,' I said, confidently, even though I was hearing the name Dr Mehrotra for the first time myself.

'Oh okay, tell him Debashish said hi,' he replied, smiled and left.

I took a sigh of relief and looked in Roy's direction once again. He was still nowhere in sight. I decided to walk in, where he was. I looked around, and spotted Roy standing in front of a rack.

'What are you doing?'

'Check this out,' Roy said with a huge grin on his face.

I went and saw the white coloured powder in the bags that were kept in front of Roy. I wanted to excitedly punch the air; this was the first step of success in this crazy pursuit. But we still had to get out of here, which was the difficult part.

Roy picked a packet and motioned me to leave. But I didn't move. I picked another bag and gave it to Roy. And picked two more bags for myself.

'Dude! Really now? Four fucking bags?!'

'Yeah, I'd need them.''

'Are you planning to get half the city high on Meth?'

'No. It would be a hit and trial method, Roy. I am pretty sure I won't be able to make it work in one go. I am accounting for wastages too.'

'But you are increasing the risk four times by doing that!'

'It's either four bags or none at all. And anyway, one bag or four, what is the difference?'

'The difference is that if they lose one bag, they blame the care taker. But if four bags go missing, they will be after our lives. They might even report a burglary or something.'

Roy succumbed after some fight, especially in the arena we were standing in. He was too nervous to argue any more. We picked the four bags and rushed out of the storage area faster than I thought was possible.

Vandana was waiting for us in the car. We weren't spending any second more than we had to in that company campus with the pseudoephedrine on us. I hugged Roy back. That was an important hug. With that hug, I felt all the negativity between us gone forever. We were back to being the Samar-Roy duo that we were known to be.

Vandana and I were on the road once again, waiting for our next adventure, which wasn't very far. I checked my watch. It was five already. By the time we would reach home, we would have only enough energy to cook dinner and doze off. The sixth day out of the ninth was also over. From here onwards, the only part left was the actual cooking of these ingredients. And come to think of it, the toughest part had just begun.

* * *

Vandana seemed different ever since she had told me her story. She seemed very detached from everything around her. It was as if she had been pretending until then and having come out of the veil freed her of all such strings.

Another thing that did was it made me feel too small. I felt my worries were too inconsequential. Whatever I worried about made me feel immature. It definitely changed my whole perspective of life.

By the time we reached, it was dinner time but we didn't have the energy to even sit at a restaurant and wait for the food to be served. We decided to go back to the flat, and just doze off.

I said goodnight to Vandana and then went to my room, changed into my night clothes and turned the light off. Just then, I heard a knock on the door. Vandana walked in. There was something different about her today. It was as if she was finally letting her insecurities come out. It was as if her loneliness was surfacing and becoming an issue for her.

She held my hand and accompanied me to the bed. She hugged me as we slept off, like a mother protecting her child from all the evil there is. I felt warmth which can melt the strongest of metals.

I Didn't Have All Day

My eyes fell on the phone. The green LED on the top meant I had a missed call. There were four and it was Aradhya's, the girl from the publishing house. It couldn't have been good news.

'Hello?' she said, when I called her back. 'Samar, where are you? I called you so many times like an hour back!'

'I was sleeping. What happened?'

'Well, I have news. And hope you are in Delhi.'

'Why? What happened?'

'I got a call from one of my friends telling me that the party is now tomorrow evening, eighth of July instead of ninth. It's in a house in Civil Lines. Ronnie called me this morning. He would have never cared to call me to tell me that there's a change in dates but it seems he really needs some Meth in this party. Do you understand what that means?'

'What?'

'That you cannot mess this up now.'

'What did you say?'

'I told him that you have good stock and you won't disappoint.'

'Don't worry. Everything is under control,' I lied, with my body almost getting numb from fear.

'Are you sure?'

'Yes, yes.'

'I'll see you tomorrow night then.'

'Bye.'

My head started whirling when I hung up.

On one side, there was Vandana, whose cancer was deteriorating every day. On the other side, there was Navya, who was sprinting towards moral and physical decay. On one side, I had a broad timeline as to how much time Vandana had. On the other side, Navya was one wrong step away from being lost forever.

But I had made my choice. Navya was living in way too dangerous a world. She would have to be saved first. And then, I will leave no stone unturned to save Vandana. Every passing minute was a reminder that I didn't have all day. I needed to be quick.

* * *

'So what is the plan now?' Vandana asked me.

It was ten in the morning. We had all the ingredients with us, in the flat itself. And yet, there was such a long way to go, with so little time. Weeks of planning had boiled down to this. For days I had been thinking Meth, how to cook it, where to get the material from, where to get the equipment, what if something went wrong, etc. But this was the big morning.

I went for a quick shower and when I came out, Vandana was not on the bed. She must have gone to her room, I thought. I slipped into a neat T-shirt and went to Vandana's room.

'So how do we go about it,' Vandana said, when I entered her room.

'Well, I wanted to do a few experiments before getting down to the real process. I wanted to know how a few chemicals work. But there seems to be no time. So we will basically divide the process into two parts.'

'And what are those?'

'We will carry out the process as a test first. We will take just a small quantity, and do it at a low scale in the first go, so that if it goes wrong, we wouldn't have wasted any raw materials. And then, when the little quantity comes out right, we will go all-in in the next round and cook all we can.'

'And considering we have two days, how many try runs can we take before making the final thing?'

'Just one.'

* * *

By eleven thirty, we were outside the Chemistry Lab, which was going to be the place where we would do it. I knew that our lab had everything that we needed. What I didn't know was that how were we going to go in and be there for two days.

There was an assistant who took care of the labs during vacations. Some professors were supposed to carry out their research projects in the labs during the vacations. But they seldom used to turn up and the lab assistants were left idle with two long months of coming and opening these labs with almost no visitors.

I was a bit worried that the lab may not be open because the assistants weren't accountable to anyone during the vacations. But it was.

'So can we just walk into this lab?' Vandana asked me.

'Well, we will have to think of a pretext,' I said, more to myself.

'So what is the profile of this *lab assistant*?'

'Well, she must be in her early twenties too. She is fair and but not sophisticated, probably stays in Shahbad Dairy, a local village. Nobody cares much about her here, but I feel she must be respected back in her village, with a government job and all,' I said.

I knew what was to follow. Vandana had a naughty smile on her face. I knew that in a few minutes, I would be throwing some random pickup line at her.

'You are going to make me go and say something corny to her, aren't you?'

'I am so tempted to make you do that but that would be risky. I have a much safer idea, which will have a much better chance of working.'

There was an audible and genuine sigh of relief from my mouth.

* * *

We waited outside for a while. Vandana wanted to have a good sight of her before we walked in.

A few minutes later, the Lab Assistant walked out. I could see from Vandana's reaction that she had been waiting to get an eyeful of her. The assistant was wearing glasses and had visibly knitted brows that day; bad mood. Vandana was observing her closely.

'Well, it seems I made a good decision. This one would have been hard to charm for you,' she softly murmured.

Even though I agreed, I took a teeny bit of offense as well.

'I mean she doesn't seem very open to mingling with anyone. We would have to handle her my way.'

'And you can tell all that by just looking at her from this distance?' I asked.

'Years of experience,' Vandana smiled.

* * *

The lab's door was open, with just the lab assistant Ashima present.

'Hello ma'am,' I said to her, with a nod of my head.

'Hello,' she replied in a suspicious voice, relishing the little joys of power her position gave her.

'Ashima ma'am, this is Vandana ma'am. She has just joined as the Head of Department for Chemistry Department. I was just telling her how well versed you are with everything in this lab.'

'Head of Department? What happened to Khanna sir?' Ashima asked.

'Oh, he has moved to some other college,' I replied.

'Oh okay,' she said. And began a guided boring tour for her new super boss. I was just hoping she doesn't throw any questions at Vandana, because she knew as much about Chemistry as I knew about French. But it seemed to be shaping alright.

And once the tour was done, Vandana looked at me.

'Very impressive laboratory you have here. Ashima seems quite experienced as well. As for the complex and challenging experiment I told you Samar, I shall sit here as you get down to it.'

Vandana took the professors chair, as I looked at Ashima from the corner of my eye to see how she was taking it. Thankfully, she didn't suspect any foul play. She bought every word of what we had said. Vandana in her suit looked like a professor and she learnt to talk like one too.

Ashima went into her small cabin, as I wondered what she did there sitting alone, in the pigeon box. Meanwhile, I went out to my car and brought all the stuff that we were carrying. It took me three rounds to carry enough stuff for one test experiment. I wondered what would happen if the test went alright and we had to do the final thing.

Finally, after a week of rigorous effort, it was time for action. I began at about one in the afternoon. I had four hours until five o'clock when the lab would officially close down.

I took the powdered pseudoephedrine and mixed it with red phosphorus and hydriodic acid. I meticulously filtered out red phosphorus, and neutralized the remaining acid. And then I drained liquid Meth carefully.

It may or may not seem like a bunch of easy steps as I list them out here, but in reality, each step was a headache. Measurements had to be perfect. I had to make sure foreign particles did not into the ingredients, both, which were being cooked and the ones which were kept on a side. I had to set up complex apparatus to carry out the whole thing. I was fast getting mentally exhausted. And the time deadline did not help either.

Just when I was passing Hydrogen Chloride gas into liquid Meth, Ashima came to us from her cabin. I had been in deep concentration all day and had lost absolute track of time. Only when she disturbed me I realized that it was evening already.

'It's time to close the lab Samar, I'm sorry,' Ashima said.

I looked at Vandana, who was half dozing all this while, and she was as clueless as I was. I realized I couldn't leave this for her.

'Ashima, we need half an hour more and then we can leave,' I said.

Ashima looked at Vandana and Vandana smiled at her. This was Ashima's opportunity to make an impression on her HoD. She smiled back and turned and started walking towards her room.

I went back to bubble Hydrogen Chloride gas. And rushed through the final few steps.

At the end of it, I filtered the solution though a residue cloth, which left behind dried Meth on the filter. Now the only step left was the crystallization of this residue. This was a slow and long process. So I set up everything and went and kept it in my car. Once I was back, I told Ashima that we were done.

Ashima gave a smile which inevitably said that she wasn't very comfortable staying back till late.

I went to the car and took care of the crystals. I expected they would take two or three hours to settle completely. So I could finally take a bit of a breather after spending so many hours in deep concentration.

Vandana ran her hand through my hair to comfort me. I looked at the dish on the backseat, with Meth on it. I felt a bit nervous. I really needed this to be alright.

As far as I could see, the process hadn't gone alright. I was way too under confident. And I had made many small mistakes which could eventually add up to be a big problem. In fact, I would be surprised if things fell in place after so many errors.

So three hours later, when we finally saw the result, I wasn't surprised at all. We had got a fine white powder instead of crystals. If I were to take these to Ronnie, he would shoot me in the head.

I went to Vandana's room to show her what was made. Just before knocking I noticed a sound coming from her room. It was the sound of sobbing.

I waited for a little while. Behind those cheery eyes and vibrant personality, there was a lonely forty year old woman, whose body was fast decaying because she had no money for a treatment. She was in pain.

As I finally entered, I caught her wiping her eyes. But I decided to act as if nothing was off. The more I would have talked about it, the more it would have depressed us. For now, we needed this distraction.

'The crystals didn't come,' I told her and barged out of the room. She looked like someone who needed time by herself.

I came back to my room and booted my laptop. The little traffic that I had managed to build on *savevandana. com* was now gone. The account had crawled over the one thousand mark. I had to come up with something bigger and better. And faster.

* * *

Days can get frustrating and disappointing at times. But something came over me when I saw those numbers on my laptop just minutes after I had seen that my whole day at the lab was also a waste. I thought I was a calm and balanced person. But on that day, as I threw around stuff in my room, punched the wall, and did a few other crazy things to vent out, discovering a new side of me.

At such a time, giving up seems so convenient. One is so easily tempted. I locked myself in the room and waited for the night to pass.

* * *

Breath Of Fresh Air

And then came the eighth of July, the day when all will be decided. I woke from the half sleep at five in the morning. I was jumpy and nervous. When I would go to bed again that night, life would have changed in so many ways. It was a do or die day.

The fact that the morning didn't look very different from a usual one was a bit weird. It was like, why do these people not know what is happening with me? It's soMething so crucial. And yet, the world seemed so unconcerned.

It was tough to wait till ten to reach the lab. We were there fifteen minutes before the opening time. We stood at some distance to make sure Ashima didn't know that we were waiting for her even before she got here.

'So how much stuff are you going to make?' Vandana asked me.

'I can't risk making everything today itself. The more the quantity, the greater the chance of messing it up,' I said.

'Makes sense,' Vandana replied.

Once Ashima was inside, we waited for another three minutes and then went inside.

We tried to act nonchalant, which was almost as difficult

a task as making Meth was. One loophole, one suspicion and we would have been thrown out of the lab. I waited for Ashima to settle down in her little room and once she was gone, we started our business.

I decided to be super careful today. I pledged to make sure that no contamination or foreign object goes into the experiment today. I closed the windows so that the wind won't disturb the experiment. I switched the fans off, even though the July heat was killing. I wore my lab coat. And I gave my phone to Vandana to make sure I had no distractions.

And I started the same process, which was now ingrained inside my head to the last detail. I did it slowly. It had taken me three hours to carry out the process on the previous day. Today, I had good six hours to carry it out. But the strain in my head was unsettling.

* * *

I nudged Vandana gently from her slumber. Her head was down on the table and when I came closer to her, I realized there was a faint sound of snoring too.

'Are we done?' she asked, as she rubbed her eyes.

'No. The crystals are settling down. It's two thirty. Let's go and grab some lunch,' I proposed.

'Yeah. How did it go?'

'It's hard to say. I was as careful as I could have been. But you can't say until you see the crystals in three hours' time.'

We carried the dish back to our cab and headed back to the flat for food. Both of us were way too tensed to make any conversation. We needed a period of nothingness and boring-ness to recuperate.

'By five thirty, the crystals would hopefully be ready. The junky party wasn't supposed to begin till eight,' I double checked in my head. We were free for the next three hours. It's a bit weird when adventure becomes normal. When excitement keeps happening, you get used to it. You need to look at yourself from a third person's perspective to appreciate the craziness of the events.

At five thirty, I nervously walked to the kitchen, where we had left the residue to crystallize. The moment I saw it, I knew it hadn't worked. If yesterday was bad, today was worse. The same powdered residue; more fine and hence, more useless. We were screwed. After years of making crystals in the lab, when I really needed to deliver, I could not.

Vandana spotted a drop of tear in my eye. She didn't know what to say to me. But she could see that my commendable resolve was beginning to give away.

'What will we do now? It's all come to an end. Navya is going to rot amongst those leeches now,' I said, my voice shivering because of the tears. 'I am good for nothing. All I do is kill people who love me truly. Firstly, I let go off Kanika. And now, it's Navya,' I said, almost sobbing rather than speaking, making efforts to deliver words and join sentences coherently.

'Get a hang on yourself Samar. It's just five thirty. And the real party won't start before ten or even later. We have at least one more chance.'

'You think we will cook Meth in our flat's kitchen now? You are better than this Vandana, you shouldn't talk about things you don't know,' I snapped at her.

'Take a deep breath, Samar. We will have plenty of time

to panic if things don't work. Let's spend this precious time in thinking of a way to make things work.'

'But how?'

'Let's call the cab, sit and then talk,' she said, as she started picking whatever stuff we had brought back into the flat.

Once we were in the car, I looked at Vandana as to what was next.

'We are going back to the lab,' she said.

'But why?' I asked. Vandana didn't bother to reply. Once the car was in the parking next to the lab, we sat in the car and stared at the lab for a while. There were no people now, except some guards at some distance.

'Let's go,' Vandana said, getting off the car.

'But where?'

Vandana walked closer to the lab. But she wasn't walking towards the lab door. It was of course shut now. She was walking to the other side — the back side. She stood close to the window at the back.

'If you are planning to get inside through the window, I think you are not seeing that they aren't just glass windows. There are iron windows inside those glasses,' I said sarcastically.

'I know. But look at this one. Seems like someone has deliberately left this one open this afternoon so that if someone wanted to sneak in after dark, all he would have to do is break some glass,' she replied with a smile.

She was right. One of the iron windows was actually half open.

'Just go and grab a few bricks from somewhere!' she said.

I broke the glass down and hoped that none of the guards would hear the sound. In a few seconds, I was back inside the lab where I had spent last two days. And then I realized Vandana couldn't climb inside all that easily. So I jumped outside again. And collected a few more bricks and helped her jump inside.

Vandana helped me with the torch in her phone. We couldn't turn on the lights because the guards would have definitely seen the light and stopped us. I quickly got down to business.

As I was filtering out the red phosphorus, my phone started vibrating. It was Aradhya. She had a reason to be nervous herself.

'Just one question Samar, is everything in place?'

'Oh yes Aradhya, you don't need to worry,' I lied confidently.

'Do you have the Meth with you?' she asked.

'Yeah. I have a bagful kept right in front of my eyes. And the crystals look beautiful.'

'The party will begin at ten.'

'We could get a bit fashionably late. And I know people might not wait for us, but they will wait for the Meth,' I said, cockily, to infuse even more confidence. Aradhya was satisfied with what she heard and hung up a lot more comfortable than when she had called.

I got back to the process. I poured the final solution through a filter cloth and dried the Meth that was left behind on the filter. And then came my favourite part, the part of the final crystallization.

'Do you think this will work?' Vandana asked me.

'Yes, it will,' I fake assured her too.

'How much Meth do you think we will manufacture today?'

'Just enough to get inside,' I said.

'But then, why did you get ingredients in such huge quantities?'

'I don't know. You can say there was a calculation mistake,' I lied. I didn't want her to know the real reason.

'You are one crazy fellow.'

Just then, I heard a clicking sound on the door. There was somebody unlocking the Chemistry Lab at this hour, which could have only meant one thing. We were caught.

We waited for the person to come in and decided to act nonchalant. We could have run but there was the dish in which the crystals were settling and you couldn't run with it through a window without spilling it.

A guard walked in. I quickly kept the dish with the crystals on a side, making sure they remained unaffected if something happened here.

The guard looked at us with victorious eyes.

'I have been working here for fifteen years,' the old guard said. 'All the other guards, especially the ones in the Admin Department, have caught people breaking in at night. But I never caught anyone because nobody comes to the Chemistry Lab in the day, forget about night. But today, after fifteen years I have caught two people,' he said with immense joy.

'Sir, it's my project submission tomorrow for my summer internship. It was very important I did it today,' I said.

'Do you really think I would hear your story and let you go? You are going nowhere but to the Head of Department tomorrow.'

'Hmm ok sir. Just let me wrap up this experiment and then we can go,' I said.

'Do you really think I care about your experiment?'

Vandana walked up to him and struck a conversation. I saw her sneaking in a hundred rupee note in his hand, as they exchanged a faint smile.

'Are we okay?' I asked her as she came back.

'No. But he would let us complete the experiment and then take us to the authorities.'

The guard came and stood right next to me to inspect that I was doing. Vandana was standing at some distance.

As the guard looked on, I picked my bag on my shoulder. On the gas, I had water which was being heated. In my hand, I had a fistful of red phosphorus. I looked at Vandana and she thankfully read my eyes and got the signal that it was time to run. I threw the red phosphorus into the warm water and there was a small blast on the gas. With my bag on my back, Vandana ran like there was no tomorrow, while I walked swiftly, making sure that the crystals wouldn't get disturbed too much.

The guard tried to fathom what had happened. The smoke stung his eyes, as he was blinded for a few minutes. He had left the laboratory door open behind him and Vandana and I stopped only after we had reached the car.

Once in the safety of the car, Vandana and I looked at each other. And then, we broke into laughter. As I said, I was feeling weird that evening and the gush of tension and then its release with the run, was just the trigger I needed to lift up my spirits.

'Come,' Vandana said, and extended her arms. That was when it struck me for the first time. She had that motherly warmth which made her so comforting. Just as we hugged, she started coughing, which once again brought back to my memory the fact which one can so easily forget on looking at her. 'But what did you do there?' she asked, trying to get her breath normal.

'There was water and heat in the container. I threw in red phosphorus which releases Phosphine gas, which caused the explosion.'

'But was it safe?'

'Yes, it is. All he needs is a breath of fresh air. So he'll be okay if he came out of the lab in next ten minutes. I noticed that he came out immediately after us. So yes, he is safe.'

'You little genius,' Vandana smiled.

'Thanks,' I said, inevitably flashing the broadest smile at her. And after a few minutes of laughter, the same old question hung between us. What next? Will we get the final crystals this time? Will we be able to pull this off?

'Where to?' I asked

'To your flat,' she replied.

Like A Building Needing Resurrection

I left the dish with Meth in the car itself. It was important that it is disturbed as little as possible. Instead, Vandana and I went in, and kept all the stuff. And then I took a breather, as Vandana made tea. And then we took a nap, to be woken up by the alarm clock two hours later.

I changed into my best clothes and so did Vandana. By around eleven, it was time for us to go to the car and check the crystals.

This was our final chance. If this didn't work, I would have to give up on Navya. I didn't know whether I had it in me to take that shock. As we slowly walked towards the car, I noticed that my leg was shivering, my heart was beating and my palms were sweating more than ever.

The dish was kept on the backseat. I went and opened the car gate and looked inside. Finally, the dish had crystals instead of white powder.

'Seems like we have done it,' I said to Vandana.

Vandana took the dish from my hand and picked a solid piece from it. She kept it against a street light and looked at it.

'Is this a good crystal?'

162

'It's one of the better ones I've made.'

'How good?'

'It's good enough for me to double the usual price if I was a real dealer,' I said.

'We have no time for compliments. Sit in the cab and drive to Civil Lines without wasting any more time,' she said, opening the back door of the car.

* * *

I saw Vandana observing me. On asking why, she fetched a small mirror from her bag and handed over to me. I had wrinkles on my forehead. The dark circles were extremely prominent now. The hair would have been all over the place but I had put in some effort to put them in order. But I did look a mess. I told myself this is the last night of strife. In a few hours, I would either have Navya next to me, or I would have to find a brand new way to move on in life. It seemed like an impossible task, the thought itself made me shiver.

I wondered how I would react on seeing Navya this time. And what that moment would be like. Civil Lines was just a thirty minute drive at that hour. Aradhya was waiting for us a kilometre away from the venue. She wanted to see what we had before she would let us meet Ronnie. She didn't want to risk her neck for us. If the product was bad, it was much safer to not show up.

We saw Aradhya, as she was nervously waiting for the two lunatics (that's what she probably thought of us). On seeing us, there was no hand shake or any greeting. She straight away asked me for what I was carrying. She took a small pinch of Meth and smelt it. I knew that she couldn't judge how good or bad it was like that.

163

'You're sure this stuff is good? Because the guy at the gate is going to check and he's an expert.'

'Vandana says it's the best stuff she has ever seen,' I said.

Aradhya looked at Vandana. Somehow she didn't look like someone whose opinion Aradhya could trust.

'I'd love to know how you got this but not today. Let's go for now,' she said, as she sat on the backseat. 'Why does your car smell funny?' she asked.

Vandana and I exchanged a goofy smile.

And then we reached the place which had been hyped to death in our heads. It was a standalone house on a rather nondescript street. You could have missed it easily but for a weird looking man outside.

That seven foot tall man at the gate looked at us and I wondered how hard he was suppressing the urge of saying what his facial expressions said, that he wanted to eat us up.

'Where are you kids headed?' he said. He couldn't have been more condescending. Thankfully, Aradhya offered to take control.

'Hi, Ronnie. I am Aradhya, Navya's friend? This is Samar. He talked to you about getting Meth for the party today.'

Ronnie asked me for a sample. He lit a pipe and smoked a part of the sample. It took him just a few seconds to judge the quality of Meth. Vandana, Aradhya and I held our breaths for those odd 30 seconds.

He liked it.

And Ronnie became a different person from that moment on. He dropped the tough contour and almost graciously welcomed us inside. He probably loved it.

We entered and we were amazed with what we saw. On the ground floor, half the Indian television industry was present. No wonder this party was so hard to enter. I kept on forgetting that even Navya was a little famous now, which brought her to such parties. I spotted some faces from Bollywood too. It seemed a little unreal and hard to swallow to witness those celebs partying so casually like that.

The place wasn't extremely posh for the gathering. But the people and the atmosphere made the ordinary place look jazzy and vibrant from inside.

On any other day, I would have wanted to soak in the ambience of that place. It smelt of smoke and there was alcohol and syringes and rolling paper wherever you looked. But we had to look around for Navya. All three of us knew how she looked. I told Vandana and Aradhya to look for her downstairs and I made my way upstairs.

If the place looked unkempt on the ground floor, then the first floor was plain broken. A little worse than Edward Norton's Fight Club house. The doors seemed rotten and the place was a mess, reeking a repulsive smell; of junkies, their body odour and that the rotting drugs. Once I was upstairs, I saw humans who seemed no better than animals. Guys and girls were lying around, semi-naked or with clothes which hadn't been washed for years. These people had religiously dedicated their lives to drugs.

There was no music here and I don't think they cared about it. It was plain pathetic.

It was hard to focus on the purpose in hand. My mind went back to the promise I had met to Swamiji. I would help everyone I could. And the only reason I managed to stop myself was because I didn't know *how* to help all these doomed people. Some of them had blisters on their body the kind Meth addicts have. I saw a young guy smile and the horrific stains on his teeth would give sleepless nights to any onlooker. I had seen all this on YouTube in the west and I was indifferent to it. But I probably wasn't prepared for such a scene in India. I was seeing it in people who were my age, who could do things to make themselves and their parents proud. It was appalling.

But right under the undercurrent of this city, they call the 'Capital', are places like these where there is more Meth in the air than oxygen, where sex seems like the obvious step after two strangers get introduced and get high together. Not that I held anything against occasional indulgences but this kind of hedonism made my head spin.

With my eyes, I was looking for Navya. But with my mind, I was hoping she is not there, not amongst these people.

I opened a few creaky doors. I looked in the balcony. But it was in the last room that I spotted DJ Vyk, with a few of his friends. I was tempted to walk up to him, punch him and ask him where Navya was. But rationality was important that emotion. So I decided to go downstairs and bring along Vandana and Aradhya.

With them, we came back to where I had spotted DJ Vyk, with his bunch of friends. Three of his friends seemed conscious, while other two would make zombies insecure. I went to the other side and looked closely, and realized that one of the dead looking persons was actually Navya. The sight of her numbed me for a complete good minute. She looked as if she had been lying there forever. It seemed that people around her had gotten used to seeing her lifeless body lying there. My heart began to sink. The guys around her were crazy enough to not notice if anything was to happen to her.

Vandana called me to the other corner of the room. I told her what I had in mind: I wanted to punch those guys and pick Navya and just leave. Vandana didn't like the idea.

'See Samar, these are Meth heads. Can I give you a piece of advice which you would keep in your head for the rest of your life?'

'Yes?'

'Never punch a Meth head. You will be surprised with what you will see. They will go insane if you will hit them, especially if they are five of them together. If picking fights with sober people is dangerous, then getting involved with these people is like a death wish.'

'You know what my next question is going to be. Do you have a better idea?'

'Yes. See, it's not a punch that a Meth head is scared of. Now ask me, what is a Meth head scared of?'

'What?' Aradhya and I asked in chorus.

'He is scared of being caught by family. And you have no idea how submissive these Meth heads become in front of family.'

'But what the hell is the plan?' I asked, getting impatient. Navya was lying lifelessly in front of my eyes. And I had to bypass these idiots to reach her.

'The plan is simple, Samar. I will be Navya's mother and Aradhya will be her sister. We will go together and shout at them. They will have absolutely no idea how to react. And then, you can come in and pick her up, and we will walk straight out of the party. Nobody will stop us. There cannot be a smoother plan to get her out of here.'

Vandana plunged in straightaway, with jaws clenched and fists curled. Her stride was brought to an abrupt end as she halted midway and gave a nasty stare across the room, as if surveying everyone. Her eyes red and bulging in anger; it was such a stellar performance!

She walked in and only one sound was audible on the whole floor. She rained abuses in Punjabi to nobody in particular. When she saw Navya, she broke into a fountain of fake tears. She cursed all the guys around her for doing this to her. Everyone, visibly shaken by now, was looking at each other, asking each other through eye contacts, 'Dude, do you have the least bit of the fucking idea of what this lady is going on about?!'

Meanwhile, she continued to sob and wail and curse God for making her see that moment. And when Aradhya joined Vandana in her tears and wailing, the Meth heads gave in. With all those drugs having replaced their neurons, it was way beyond their comprehension now. Dj Vyk was too stunned to come up with a meaningful explanation. He was trying to rack his brain which was functioning at thirty percent efficiency at that time. He had no prior knowledge about Navya's family and he wasn't able to understand an iota of the punjabi abuses were being hurled at him. He just stood there, blinking eyes like a pigeon, contemplating if this was the worst Bad Trip he's been on.

'We are taking her with us,' Vandana announced, like a headmistress with an invisible spanking rod in her hand. This was my cue to step in.

That was the most nervous walk of my life. On one

side, I was scared that this Meth heads will figure out our lie and beat us to death. On the other side, the sight of Navya was making me jittery; I was approaching her lifeless unconscious body. I feared walking up to her and realizing she had no pulse. What if an overdose of Meth had taken her us from us? I was sweating, I was shivering. And if I were speaking I would have stammered too.

I walked up to Navya and turned her over. I flinched on seeing the terrible condition her face was in and extended a hand to check her pulse. It seemed alright. I left a sigh of relief.

'What's wrong with her?' I asked a junkie rolled next to her.

'She is in a long sleep,' he said, casually.

'I can see that. But why?'

'Well, she has scored too much this week.'

'But I thought Meth makes you sleepless, doesn't it?'

'Yes, it does. It makes you go days without sleep. But when that period ends, you go in a long sleep, like she has.'

'So when will she wake up?'

'My guess is day after tomorrow, but you can never tell.'

I picked Navya without thinking anything now. She had always been slim but had grown increasingly lighter now. Her pungent smell hit my nostrils. She needed a bath, her mouth needed washing and her hair needed detangling.

Vandana and Aradhya led the way like an enraged mother and a furious sister, as I climbed the stairs behind them, with Navya in my arms. We walked through the crowd and the contour on our faces didn't let anyone stop us. Thankfully, Ronnie was not at the gate any more. And just like that, we walked out of the party, and walked up to our car and I kept Navya in the back seat. She collapsed there like a bag of rice.

We quickly sat in our seats and within the next few minutes, we were out of Civil Lines. We dropped Aradhya to her house and thanked her profusely.

Once Vandana and I were on the main road, the mood of the car changed. Navya was in a terrible condition and Vandana's cancer was growing as fast as ever but still, we had achieved something. Navya was with us and we could at least take care of her. I looked at Vandana and wondered what is going to do in celebration.

I thought she might turn on the music really loud or maybe sing herself. Or maybe she would high five and flash a broad smile. But what I saw surprised me.

Vandana let out a loud cry. And I saw a drop of tear leave her left eye. She didn't stall her emotions. She let it flow. And she cried some more.

* * *

Once we were home, I carried Navya to Vandana's room and dropped her there. I wanted to hug her good night but I decided against it. I wanted to hug her when she would hug me back.

Vandana and I stood in her room, and looked at her in deep sleep.

'She's like a building in the need of resurrection Samar. And you are a single labourer. It might seem like an impossible task, but more impossible things have been done before.'

I didn't respond. And instead kept looking at Navya. The first thing you noticed about her face was her dark circles. Then puffy eyes. And her lips, which had gone dry as if she hadn't moisturized them since years.

From a gorgeous enigmatic girl that I had known her to be, she was a now like a disfigured painting, with all the colour sapped out of it.

Vandana slept on my bed and I slept on the floor. As I stared in darkness of the night, there was only one question going through my head.

What if she wakes up and slaps me and leaves?

* * *

Showing Very High Confidence

Even though I felt I had already done a lot of work, the next morning I knew that having come so far, the real work began from here. It was the ninth of July.

Vandana and I were standing in the balcony, where we did most of our chit chatting.

'So this is what it settles down to. We have her body. But would we be able to have Navya, the person?' I asked.

'It depends on you, Samar. If you take good care of yourself, I believe you can bring her back to life.'

'Hmmm.'

'Tell me more about her. Where does she come from? What are her roots? How is her family? Have you met them?'

'I had seen a glimpse of her dad when he had come to Woodstock Village in Goa to take Navya back home. And I thought he must be an extremely strict dad. In fact, that might be the reason why Navya felt so desperate to break away.'

'You have his phone number?' Vandana asked me. I didn't like the question. Definitely, Vandana didn't expect me to call Navya's dad.

172

'I don't,' I said, not wanting to know what Vandana had in mind.

'But Joseph, your guy at Woodstock would have it no?'

So she forced me into calling Joseph, make the small talk and give him a convincing reason for needing Mr Sharma's number. Joseph was a sweet guy and I didn't think he would say no to me for anything.

'Now call Mr Sharma and tell him to come to Delhi,' Vandana said, firmly.

'Are you out of your mind?!' I reacted.

'I am in complete control of my mind. Call Mr Sharma to Delhi right now. You kids think you know everything. We need an adult man's brain to handle this situation. Call him right now, Samar,' Vandana said.

'Listen Vandana, you have not seen Mr Sharma but I have. I have heard stories of him from Navya. He is not someone who would see his daughter in this condition and try to sympathize. He is someone who would *disown* his daughter, probably slap her and storm out on seeing her in this condition.'

Vandana didn't like my argument.

'How many daughters have you fathered?'

'It's not about that. I know how he thinks. Take my word for it!'

'You don't know a parent's heart, Samar. Navya is just . . . ill. All she needs is some love, some care and some medicine. And she will be okay. Give me his number, I will call him,' Vandana said.

I listened as Vandana narrated the situation to Mr Sharma. He didn't react too much on the phone. Instead, he told Vandana that he will take the first flight to Delhi. It was twelve in the afternoon right now. I knew he would be here before dark.

And in the meantime, I engrossed myself on YouTube, into videos on how to bring a Meth addict back to life. I read articles and articles on what to do and what not to do. I kept a notebook by my side and made notes. It was as if it was becoming the most ambitious task of my life.

But I was determined. If hard work was what it required, I was more than willing to give it.

* * *

When the doorbell rang at six o'clock, I knew it would be Mr Sharma, Navya's dad. Navya was still out of her senses and looked pretty unwell. Vandana went and opened the door.

Mr Sharma walked in and when Vandana asked him for tea or water, he plainly said, 'Where is she?'

I could see a father's restlessness written all over his stern face. He hadn't seen her in months and how disconcerted he was with the way she had turned out. Maybe there was hope. Maybe he would be on our side.

Vandana took him inside, where Navya had been sleeping. Mr Sharma walked in and saw his daughter in that broken condition. He was devastated with what he saw. His initial reaction was of anger. This was what I had feared. I wasn't very excited about what was to follow. He was capable of anything. He could hold us responsible for what had happened. He could insist on taking her back to Indore and locking her in a room for months. He could disown her completely.

But then I saw the anger giving way to the love of a father. He didn't say anything but his eyes revealed every thought going through his head, as his expression transformed from one to another.

And then he walked out of the room, without saying anything. He sat on the couch, gathering his thoughts, still in deep concentration. 'Tell me from the beginning, precisely everything,' he said.

Vandana took a step forward and she began to tell the story like a mother tells the story of her daughter. There was so much empathy in her voice when she spoke that one could feel her love for Navya even though she was yet to properly meet her.

The story ended. There was a tear or two in the eyes of more than one person in that room. It was clear by now that my initial judgment of him being a ruthless and tyrannous man had been utterly wrong. He was, as Vandana had assured, a loving father who wanted to see his daughter coming back to life from being burned and broken.

'I want to start with saying thank you to the both of you. You have taken very good care of Navya and she is lucky that she has friends like you. And secondly, I want to help you in taking care of her.'

But then, he said after pondering for a while, 'I know for a fact that I will be more destructive than constructive. She might turn hostile towards me and try escaping again. I am leaving this job to you. You have my phone number. Call me whenever you want. I will not tell anything about this to her mother. And when we have our old Navya back, call me. I will come with her mother and we will

175

meet her,' he said in a voice so sombre that it could pierce through stone.

With these words, he picked the single bag that he had brought and began to from the same door from which he had entered just an hour ago. He was a man of conviction and it didn't take him very long to understand situations and make a decision.

Just as he was leaving, he looked at both of us and said, 'I'm showing very high confidence in the two of you. Don't make me regret it.'

He had shown immense confidence in us. I didn't know whether we were worthy of this confidence or not. But it definitely gave me the heart to take on this challenge.

Vandana could only be my advisor but I was the one who was to actually do it. After the evening tea, I went back to the internet and made some more notes. And once I was satisfied with the research, at around twelve in the night, with a notebook full of notes, I went up to Vandana. I showed her what I had planned. As I was explaining, I wondered whether she was listening or not. And if she was listening, whether she was understanding anything or not.

'You know what are your two biggest gifts, Samar?' she said once I was done with my rant.

'What?' I said, getting all excited in anticipation of hearing good things about me.

'Your biggest gift is that you are a great learner. I give you something to learn and tell you the reason why you have to learn and you will find a way to do it. I've known a lot of young men. But you are different. Some guys say I can't do it. Some says I will try, which actually means

I will not try hard enough. But you . ... you are just so much more accurate with whatever you do!'

'Wow! And the second?'

'The second of course is your ability to love whole heartedly, unconditionally and selflessly. When you love someone, there's nothing that you hold back. In today's world, it's a very rare virtue to have.'

I smiled. And tried not to blush. And then wondered how was this related to what I had been blabbering for like half an hour. And I think it showed on my face.

'Navya doesn't need these notes, Samar,' Vandana continued. 'This is what I would need if I was in Navya's place. But Navya is not me. *She has you.*'

'But I have no idea what she needs. I have never known anyone who has dealt with a problem like hers.'

'Be patient. We don't even know as to how she will react when she wakes up.'

'How do you think it would be?'

'I can't say yet. But I do know that her reaction will play an important role in how you should go about curing her.'

'See,' she continued, 'normally, Meth addicts show extreme withdrawal symptoms. They lose interest in everything. All they think of is Meth. And I am afraid, Navya could have gone that way.'

'Hmm. Let's just wait for tomorrow morning and see what happens,' I said.

The next day would have been an important day in my life; when I would *actually* get to meet Navya after all these months. I went to her room and looked at her asleep. I wanted to lie down next to her, cuddle her, and envelop her inside my chest. My Navya was a gypsy, a wandering soul, looking for peace. She was a misfit in this world, a much misunderstood person who was born for a different purpose.

* * *

As The Silence Got Longer

The sound was sharp and loud, of metal hitting the floor from some height. It sounded like a steel plate or glass had fallen down in the kitchen. I looked at the bed in front of me, and Vandana was fast asleep on it. So who was in the kitchen?

I got up and rubbed my eyes to adjust to the dim light. And tiptoed out of the room. The kitchen light was switched on. I entered and saw Navya standing in front of me, with a glass of water in one hand and the bottle in the other. She was drinking and spilling water all over her.

Even though she had woken up in a foreign place, she was at ease, as if she did it often. Instead of running around, trying to get a hang of where she was and how she got there, she had coolly gone to the kitchen, picked a water bottle and clumsily started drinking water.

The next moment will be etched in my memory forever. Navya's eyes fell on me. Would she recognize me? If she will, will she slap me and go away? Or will she cry and run towards me and hug me?

Her actual reaction was an anti-climax. She recognized me. But she didn't react. It was as if we had met last evening and the fact that she was in my flat had nothing unusual about it. She seemed incapable of reacting. Much weirder things had happened with her and the best she could come up with was a five second blank stare. And then she looked away. And gulped down a bottle of water.

Once she was done with the bottle in her hand, she looked at me.

'Hi Samar. How are you?' she asked, plainly.

'I am good. And I don't think I need to ask how you are.'

'What do you mean?'

'You're a mess and it's more than visible.'

She didn't react or take offense. Instead, she looked around the flat.

How did I reach here? In fact, where is *here*? I mean, where am I?'

'This is my place. I was there at your horrendous party yesterday. I couldn't believe what I saw Navya. What have you done to yourself?'

'Oh, you were at Ronnie's too? You know him? Isn't he a darling?'

Ronnie was anything but anybody's darling. Perhaps he was sweeter to pretty girls who were sort of famous.

'Yeah. I went to his party just to pick you.'

'You mean to say you just walked into a Ronnie's party, picked me and walked out?'

When she put it like that, it sounded hard to believe. I didn't want to explain the whole episode to her. The last thing you want to tell a Meth addict is that you can cook Meth.

'Did you like the party?' she asked. I looked at her and I realized the enormity of the task at my hand. Party? Really? She was almost dying there. By what definition would that be a party? She had changed completely as a person. People having Meth and other drugs was nothing out of ordinary for her now. She expected me to walk into that necropolis and enjoy myself.

'Shut up Navya! Those people were animals! May be worse.'

'Relax Samar. It's no big deal,' she said, as she walked past me into her room. As far as she was concerned, the conversation was over. She lost interest in talking to me the moment she got to know my views on that 'party'.

I followed her into her room. This conversation was definitely not over. Out of all the terrible possibilities on seeing Navya, I hadn't considered this one. That she would meet me and it would nothing major for her. And now, I was overwhelmed all over again.

I walked up to Navya, and held her by her arms. And I looked deep into her eyes. This was the only way I could get her attention. And with all the conviction in the whole of my body, I told her, 'Meth is poison, Navya. Stop punishing and abusing your body.'

She looked at me, as if I had just slapped her or something.

'What is wrong with you?' she said. 'Who the fuck are you to decide what is good and what is bad, what is right and what is wrong?'

Every word coming out of her mouth was like a knife through my heart. If it was not three in the night, she would have been on her way out of house already. She belonged to a different world now.

Her comment wasn't worthy of a response. As far as she was concerned, I was being a kid. I could see that she was absolutely and completely detached from everything around her. I looked into her unfocussed, disoriented eyes, and I knew what was happening: She was undergoing a drug craving.

She didn't care about what was happening around her. Her thoughts were completely focussed on how to find the drug again, how to get back to it. I could see that we couldn't have waited till the morning; she needed immediate attention.

So I took her back to my room, where she had slept. I made her sit down on the bed and looked at her in her eyes.

'If you want to go back to that gutter, Navya, I won't stop you. It's your life and you have every right to decide how you want to spend it. But before you go, I want you to listen to me for half an hour. If you still want to go after that, I will drop you wherever you want me to. '

I maintained a serious face trying to deliver the seriousness in what I was saying. But Navya had a faint smile on her face, as she chewed on what I had said.

'See Samar, there was a point, when if you would have told me to jump off the train with you, I would have done that at the blink of an eye. I was yours and I would have done anything for that extra second spent with you. But that moment is gone. That phase is over. You weren't available to me then, and now, the ship has left the yard. I am not returning.'

So this was what it was about. Drugs were her rebound after whatever she felt for me in Goa.

I could feel my nerves pulsating at the side of my forehead. So was it my fault again? After this, I didn't have strength left myself to give her strength. I asked her to go to sleep for now, with a baseless confidence that she would be there when we woke up.

* * *

I looked around, in her room, in her washroom, out in the balcony, but she had left. I looked for a note but there was none. Vandana woke up soon after. She didn't know about my conversation last night with Navya but she figured out that Navya had left by the look on my face, even without looking around.

Just then, the doorbell rang. Such a gush of mixed emotions sprung up. With every step that I took towards the door, my thoughts kept flipping. It could be her, it was not her.

And it was her. As she stood there, she had no idea how scared we had got when she was not there in her room. She had bought a loaf of bread and a butter bar.

'You guys don't eat bread?' she said, as she walked in. And when she said, *you guys don't get bread*, she had not just said that. She had said a lot of things. She had said that she was going to stay with us. I believe it was a game for her, which she wanted to play. I didn't know whether she wanted to quit drugs or not. And even though she didn't mean a lot of things she had said last night, I had a feeling she didn't see what was wrong with drugs yet. But just the fact that she had agreed to stay was a mini victory. It meant there was a lot of work ahead of us but at least we will get a chance.

I had had a restless night but she was there now. I exchanged a congratulatory look with Vandana but she wasn't there last night. Vandana didn't know how scared I had got after talking to Navya.

Navya nonchalantly walked into the kitchen and started making tea.

'She's wonderful,' Vandana whispered to me softly. *She wasn't wonderful last night,* I felt like telling her but abstained.

'All she needs a good bath,' Vandana added. After making the tea, Navya came and sat on the table and had a few slices with butter, as we looked on. Once she was done, I went to my room, leaving Vandana and Navya alone.

* * *

The bath had done her a lot of good. It had seemed like a thorough bath and finally, I could see that out of all the marks on her body and face, which ones were more permanent than the others. Her hair had lost its lustre. But she smelled much better after the shower.

It was the eleventh of July. In twenty days' time, I had to go back to college. Vandana's cough and pain were worsening with time. And Navya needed the smallest of triggers to go back to how she was. If there was one thing we didn't have, it was time. I wanted to sit with Navya and talk to her about drugs.

I sat with her in my room. I had collected some stuff on my laptop that I wanted to make her watch. I started with showing her how people look after a few years of Meth consumption. How their skin gets patchy, their hair becomes skimpy and their teeth rot away. They become skinny in an unhealthy way and begin to an abusive, restless and crazy in the head after a while. I showed her how it makes people get into crime for money, and do all sort of heinous acts. She listened to me attentively even though I wasn't convinced that I was getting through to her. But as I went on, I made sure I maintained eye contact with her to make her realize the seriousness of this.

Once I was done, it was time for her verdict, that whether she was convinced or not. She didn't seem in deep thought which suggested she had made up her mind.

It seemed as if she was toying with me and mentally laughing at the seriousness with which I was taking it.

As the silence got longer and so did the smile on her face, I waited for the next words to come out of her mouth. With the naughtiest smile I had seen on her, she said just one word.

'Relax.'

* * *

Waiting For Death
In A Flat, Alone

Navya and I were standing in the balcony, watching the sun go down over the buildings in front of us. She hadn't seen this flat before but had heard tens of stories about it the last time we had met. As the sunlight began to fade, Navya's initial resolve seemed to be wavering. Her voice wasn't as unwavering as it was in the morning and her body movements were a bit jumbled up. I knew what was happening. Her craving for drug was coming back, little by little. And I couldn't really blame her because an urge for drugs is something physiological. When someone has been using drugs for so long, their urge for it almost becomes out of their own control.

She was transiting between becoming extremely quiet to extremely agitated without any trigger. Her conversations were a bit abstract too now.

'What did you think the first time you saw me?' she asked.

'I thought you were the kind of person I should never get to know.'

'Then why did you get to know me?'

'Why do you ask?' I said.

'Because sometimes I wish it would have been so much better if you had gone by that gut and had not known me.'

'Why are you so hard on yourself?' I asked.

'Because I'm such a mess.'

'But I love your mess.'

'You know what I thought when I saw you the first time? I thought you were the kind of guy anybody could fall in love with. Which was enough for me to hate you.'

'And then what happened?' I asked.

'In a few weeks, I saw you again. And you know what I thought this time? Look at that boy, the boy with whom anybody can fall in love. I'm becoming a part of that *anybody*.'

I told her about Vandana. I wanted to tell her quickly before she misconstrues anything in her head. I didn't want Navya to make the mistake I had made of mistaking Vandana for somebody she was not.

'So what are you doing to collect the money?' Navya asked.

I told her about the website *savevandana.com*. We walked to my room and checked the numbers. One thousand, one hundred and seventy three rupees. Far from what I could use.

'I think it's time we thought of something else,' I said.

'Like what?' asked Navya, perplexed.

'If only I knew what,' I replied, dismayed.

* * *

Vandana entered the room with a tea tray in her hands and a smile on her face. Just as she kept the tray on the

187

bed, she broke into a fit of cough. She went rushing to the washroom, probably to spit out the blood she had coughed up. She didn't have much time and I knew we could soon reach a stage when no treatment will be good enough for her. It was a warm July evening and somehow, sitting with Navya and Vandana in one room, in spite of the dreary circumstances, I felt calm. It was like sitting with my family.

I thought of all three of us. Each of us was going through myriad dimensions of our struggles.

On one corner of the triangle, there was me, who had started his journey trying to get over the loss of the girl I loved. And in the process, found a completely new meaning of life.

On the second corner, there was Navya, a puppet whose master had been drugs, who, in trying to forget her bad memories had lost herself.

On the other corner, there was Vandana, the bravest of all of us, fighting for her life, with a smile on her face.

'You want to come to the temple?' Vandana asked Navya. She shook her head. I knew she wasn't the temple type. Neither was I, but Vandana didn't give me a choice. She ordered me to come with her. Also, I didn't have Navya's excuse, of being too unstable to go out.

So Vandana and I decided to go on our own.

'So what do you think?' I asked her.

'She is in a pretty bad shape. You have your work cut out.'

'What do you mean?'

'She is totally consumed by Meth. Her body is dependent on it. She needs some distraction, which will take her mind away from it. But it's not going to be easy with the condition she is in.'

I looked at Vandana as she prayed on. And then we started our return journey.

The main door was ajar when we came back. But the door of my room was locked. Perhaps Navya was sleeping or something, I thought. So we went to my room. I was reading the newspaper when my eyes fell on the cupboard in front of me. It was open, even though I remembered clearly that it was closed when we had gone. My heart skipped a beat because I had kept the remaining Meth that I had produced in the lab in that cupboard. I got up quickly and checked and my biggest fears had come true. Navya had taken a dose from the cupboard.

I ran to my room and started knocking profusely. Navya opened the door and she was visibly high. She had a naughty, annoying smile on her face. She thought it was funny. I knew there was no point shouting at her. In fact, I felt so guilty for being so stupid. I should have disposed the remaining Meth there and then.

Navya had become extremely energetic due to the drug. She was almost jumping around in excitement. She wanted to go out but we didn't let her. Now all we could do was wait for the morning till the effect of the drug would wear off.

'I think there is only one way out,' Vandana said.

'Which is?'

'She needs a change of environment. Just like you did when you went to Rishikesh. Take her out of town, where she can be happier. Where she has things to do and doesn't feel out of place.'

I looked at her. And I said, 'I know exactly what you are talking about.'

* * *

'Obviously you two have to leave for Goa at the soonest!' Vandana shouted.

'Are you serious? You really think I will leave you here in this condition?'

'And you seriously think I will let you not go to Goa because of me?' Vandana shouted louder.

'But you have to!' I shouted too this time. Vandana was taken aback. Her contour changed and she took a deep breath.

'Samar, listen to me. Through whatever threads we are bound to each other, our goals are different. We are born alone and then we take a trip through this world, where we meet amazing people, spend time with them and the part ways for death,' she said.

'Stop sermonising! I'm not going to let you wait for death in this flat, alone! '

'I haven't asked anything from you till date. All your efforts, Swamiji's hopes and my contributions will be a waste if you don't further this plan. I want to spend time in this flat alone. It'll do me good. I am in not as bad a shape as you think I am in, Samar,' Vandana reasoned.

We kept arguing for pretty long.

'There are only two scenarios in which I will leave for Goa. You will have to either get admitted into a hospital.'

'You're out of your mind, Samar.'

'Or you go back to Rishikesh.'

We kept arguing late into the night. And Vandana

finally gave in. She agreed to go back to Rishikesh, which wasn't much consolation because nobody in Rishikesh knew about her illness. On top of that, Rishikesh wasn't really famous for its hospitals.

I booked two train tickets for Goa for two days later. And another one for Rishikesh, which was for Vandana. I needed a day in Delhi to wrap up a few things I wanted to. I would have to go to Goa with Navya, to Woodstock Village, where we had first met, and re-live all those days. Take her there and love her more than she thinks I was capable of. That's what every Meth addict needs: pure unadulterated, unconditional love.

As we sat together on the final evening, the mood in the house was sombre. Navya was her usual irritable self. She was having a real tough time managing herself without the Meth. It had been two days now and this was the longest she had spent without using in a long time.

But I could see she was trying. She was being a sport about this, as she understood that this day was about Vandana and not about her. She got the gravity of the situation and decided to put her pain on the backseat.

'Samar,' Vandana said, breaking the silence which had engulfed the apartment all evening, 'I like your apartment. I think it's a good place to spend my last few days while you will be in Goa.'

'Nothing will happen to you. And you're not spending any more days in this house.'

'Not saying will not change the truth, Samar. You have a beautiful life ahead of you. There is no greater blessing than being young.'

'I know,' I said.

'No, you don't. Only the young don't know the charm

191

of being young. You have to be old and dying to really know it. And there's another thing I want to tell you.'

'What?'

'You made me understand why it is such a great feeling to be a mother. You made me understand what it means to get and give unconditional love. But probably I am lucky that I don't have any kids of my own.'

'Why?' I asked.

'Because if I did, I would be really worried what will happen to them when I die. But with Samar, I know he has a mother who cares for him a lot. So I can die in peace.'

I held her hand and tried to comfort her. And sitting there, on the floor of the living room, we went to sleep, to wake up next morning and catch the train.

And as I said good bye to her, standing on the porch, there was only one thing on my mind.

I won't let her die.

* * *

Vandana's train was two hours after ours. I was a bit worried that whether she would actually get on her train or not. But I had locked my flat and kept the key in my pocket. As Navya and I sat in our seats, Vandana waited outside.

Goodbyes are generally tough. Saying bye to Vandana was difficult on so many levels. I cried, Navya cried and so did Vandana when we said bye. But I knew it was much, much tougher for Vandana than it was for us.

We were moving to a place we liked with people we loved. But Vandana was going to be alone. It was one thing to face death, and it's a much, much bigger challenge to face it alone.

As I closed my eyes, sitting on the window seat of the train, a very scary thought crossed my mind. What if I come back and Vandana is not there. What if, she succumbs to the mental stress of waiting for her death and commits suicide?

I opened my eyes with a jerk and Vandana was standing right there, smiling at us. The train started moving and Vandana started waving at us. I noticed there was something in her hand. It was a big key. I knew what it was the moment I saw it. And she was deliberately showing it to me, telling me that she was going back to the flat as soon as the train left the platform.

Vandana took the metro for Rohini, where my flat was. As she entered the flat, she looked around. The same flat had a cheery feeling to it until a few minutes ago. She had never been alone in this flat before. But today, the silence of it was deafening for her. She looked at the walls, and she knew, she wasn't made for living alone.

Damn, she could really use a TV in the house at that time. She decided to go straight to the kitchen, and started preparing for baking a cake. She did everything really slow and tried to tire herself as much as she could, so that she would consume as much time as she could and would be tired by the night and would just doze off at night.

When the cake was done, she took a small bite. It was delicious. For a second, she was ecstatic. But then, the very next second, an unprecedented sadness gripped over her. She had nobody to share the wonderful cake with. How she wished she had Divya with her, who would tell her she was a magician to have baked such an art. How she wished she had Samar, to tell her that it was not a cake, it was edible poetry. How she wished she had Navya, who would love the cake but would not

193

react but the faint smile on her face would be worth a thousand compliments.

Vandana dreaded the next week. She somehow knew she didn't have the mental stamina to go through it. She knew it was a matter of time that she would collapse on the floor of the flat. She felt as if she had spent the forty years of her life setting herself up for this. As if she had alienated every possible support from her life, including Samar and Navya now.

Vandana tried hard but she couldn't sleep that night. She couldn't bring herself to think positive. She imagined that Samar also becomes a Meth addict and stays on with Navya in Goa. She thought of Divya, she thought about how she would react on seeing Vandana in such a condition.

When Vandana went to the washroom in the morning, she realized she had aged more in the last night than last five years combined. Lack of sleep gave her dark circles. She decided to go to the park and came back rather tired. And as she came back and sat on the dining table again, alone, she got convinced that she would never be able to sleep again. There was no reason for the belief, as baselessly as many of her other thoughts, she got convinced.

But this belief got shattered when she finally dozed off at six in the evening. She didn't sleep for long. By eleven in the night, she was back to lying down open eyed on her bed. A dry tear rolled down her right cheek. By now, she didn't know what was worse: The physical weakness, unbearable pain and incessant cough or the mental agony of being so lonely that it was fatal in itself. Or the fear of looking at death in the eye, of wondering every morning, that whether you would see the next one or not.

On the fourth morning, Vandana did collapse and fall

on the floor. Obviously, there was nobody to take care of her and even though she knew this day would come, she hadn't been able to plan for it in any way, simply because she didn't know who to call.

Around five hours later, she woke up with a sharp pain in her head. Even though she had felt unhealthy on the inside for a long time, she was now getting convinced that her end was near. She didn't have much time left. She was convinced that Samar would come back from Goa to find her ten day rotten body, with flies on it.

If only she had known things could go this wrong when she had left home at the age of eighteen. Maybe, she was made for a boring life and she hadn't been able to handle all this excitement. What all she could give up for a head massage from her mother at this point.

Really, what can be worse than waiting for death, in a flat, alone?

* * *

'Yes, This Is Me.'

In the train, Navya wasn't able to handle her edginess and uneasiness. She wouldn't sit in one place for long. And then, she wouldn't sleep all night. She was visibly perturbed all the time. She felt nauseous and claustrophobic in that little space. At every station, no matter what time of the day, she would get down and take a walk. She would look at the open air as if she was a fish who finally left under water and could finally breathe.

I just prayed that what I was trying to do was possible. Remembering Vandana made me believe that I was on the right path.

We got down from the train at Panjim and took a bus to Arambol. There is something about the air in Goa. It has the some invisible magnetic that sucks negativity out of you and making everything seem several times prettier and fresher.

It was as if her eyes were looking for just one thing. I couldn't wait to reach Woodstock. I could really use the support of my friends at Woodstock, Joseph's dominance and Imran's age old wisdom.

* * *

Nobody knew we were coming to Woodstock. Nobody had any idea what had happened after we had left. And out of the blue, we would be standing at their doorstep. But I was sure of one thing. They must have definitely missed us when we were gone.

Nothing had changed in Woodstock. In the middle there was the open area, where the parties happened. Around the vacant area, there were rooms made of thatch on three sides. There was a restaurant on the fourth side.

We started with looking for Joseph. When I saw he wasn't in his office, I knew he would be in his room. Navya and I went to his room, with our bags on our shoulders. Joseph was watching something on TV when we knocked. On seeing us, Joseph was overjoyed. Even though he was still his calm self but could read in his eyes that he was elated.

Imran's reaction was much more flamboyant. He jumped and danced and sang a line or two to welcome us. He made sure everybody knew we were back. And he made sure we knew how much he had missed us.

'It seemed you took all the joys of Woodstock with you when you left,' he said, hugging us.

'I will cook your favourite arabiatta pasta and pepperoni pizza,' Imran said. He then escorted us to our rooms, as instructed by Joseph. Navya's room was two rooms away from my room. I felt a bit uneasy about it, even though her room was only a few steps away from my room. I was not comfortable with letting Navya away of my eye for even a few hours. Navya needed constant attention and even the smallest of lapses could be highly damaging for her.

I settled my stuff in my room and went for a shower,

as we had been in the train for a day. Once I was done, I knocked on Navya's door. When she didn't answer to the knock, I assumed she must be having a shower and I went for a walk on the beach and around Woodstock. It was a nostalgic walk down the amnesia lane.

I came back to Navya's room around sunset. It seemed the concept of time wasn't relevant in this place. There were no offices to attend or classes to reach. I knocked on Navya's room once again.

She opened the door this time. She stood in front of me. Clearly, she had not taken a shower, probably because she had stopped seeing a point in them. She seemed tired and restless. I pitied her condition too; she was trying so hard to fight her craving off. Thankfully, the party was about to begin at Woodstock. And it turned the mood around completely.

For the first time, the Woodstock people were partying harder than the guests were. Imran got high till the point where his cooking skills weren't getting impaired. Joseph was as drunk as he could be, making sure that no one else was sober.

Navya and I were in the middle of all this. In the beginning I was ecstatic. I hadn't experienced a happy-high in a long while and there are things you can only do in Goa.

But then I observed Navya. Nothing had changed for her: Her eyes were unfocussed and her lips were forcefully stretched into a smile. I had been euphoric from my decision to come to Goa. It all melted that moment.

* * *

In the month of July, the Village had few guests, as it was an off season. The next morning, I woke up with a mild hangover. I felt like discussing what was bothering me with someone. And there was only one man I could think of: Imran.

His cheery and jumpy body adorned a stilted demeanour now. My guess – terrible hangover. But he smiled at me when he saw me. There was something going through his head. I believed I knew what it was.

'What is wrong with Navya?' he asked me without any preamble, as I sat in the chair in front of him.

And I began the story. I told him what had happened after Kanika passed away. And about The Ashram and then how I had found Navya again. And in what condition.

'It's no big deal, Samar. We have dealt with much bigger issues than Meth. I am sure we will get her alright.'

I looked at him and he must have seen how unsure I was. He pressed my hand to comfort me but I knew we had to push the 'Sisyphus' rock up the mountain and let it not roll back.

'I have known some drug heads. And I think drugs might change, the treatment remains the same. And the point is distraction. She should be so engrossed in doing what she loves, that she forgets her addiction.'

'How do we go about it?'

'If she loves painting, we make sure she paints. If she loves singing, we make sure she sings. If she loves running, we make sure she runs. You get the crux, right?'

'Yes, I do,' I said.

'Also, it's important that we make sure she is tired by the end of the day. Only then she will sleep well. Or otherwise, she would have tough nights. All drug addicts have sleep issues.'

I couldn't agree more. Just then, Navya stepped out of her room.

Imran was prepared for her. As she walked in, Imran got up from his chair and walked up to her.

'Navya, do you see any change in me since you left?'

Navya looked at him top to bottom. Imran was a blob of fat, with little hair on his head. He always wore a white vest, with no shirt on, with a sarong, or a *lungi* at the bottom. He looked like someone whom you wouldn't want as your cook. But luckily, looks weren't really a criteria for a cook, as they seldom go in front of the guests.

'Well, I think you have become even more curvaceous than you were before,' Navya joked.

'Yeah. But I think I could lose a few grams,' Imran blushed.

'Yeah, you totally could. All you need is some will power and a good trainer.'

'I have plenty of will power and I think you are the best trainer I can ever get,' Imran said.

I could see what he was doing there. His plan was to make Navya make him work out. And in the process she would have to work hard too. We knew that Navya will never work out for herself. But she could definitely work out with Imran.

Imran had always been the sidekick of Woodstock. He would quietly go about his work without being a pain in anybody's ass. This often made people forget how intelligent he was.

As Navya smiled and went to her room to change to her track pants and put on a hair band, I felt better about my decision of coming to Woodstock.

Enjoying a lazy brunch with Joseph, we watched Imran and Navya leave for the beach for a jog. We realized we needed to make a daily schedule for Navya, making sure she is occupied with happy thoughts, surrounding with things she likes to do. This afternoon, she would 'accidentally' come across a canvas and some colours. She will brush past books, which we knew she would want to read. She would come across pen and paper which would make her want to write. She would bump into interesting people, with whom she would want to have a conversation.

When Navya and Imran came back, Imran announced, hardly coherent because he was trying to catch his breath, that courtesy Navya, he needed to lie down for the next seventy two hours. Joseph went after him to tell him that he didn't have more than two hours before he got back to work.

That left Navya and me alone. She was sweaty too, from the run. She had her unwound her hair to allow them to dry down. I knew what was next. It was time to revive our walks on the beach. That was how we connected the last time. With her on one of my side, and the sea on the other side, I believed that the world was complete.

'So what went so wrong, Navya? How did it reach where it did? Why did you go so far on this path? Didn't you realize what atrocious harm you were doing to yourself and everyone who ever loved you?' I said.

'You won't understand. When things go as wrong as they had with me, people can do strange things.'

'But tell me what happened. You left Goa with your dad without leaving any way for us to trace you. And the next time I saw you, you were slightly better than a dead body in Urban Pind, with a scumbag who calls himself DJ Vyk.'

Navya looked down. I think she was contemplating where to begin. The beach must have done her mood a lot of good.

'My dad took me straight to Bhopal from Goa. He locked me up in a room and told me that my studies were done. He loved me and all, but he believed that I was too unstable for college and would end up harming myself. He is my dad and he turned out to be right. I did end up harming myself eventually.

I ran away from the house at the first chance I got. DJ Vyk was my senior in college and we had been friends when he was in school. And somehow, I had kept in touch with him after school because at the back of my mind I had known that if someday I had to escape to Delhi, his house would be a strong possibility. Well, I did come to Delhi and landed up at his doorstep, without options it was understood that we were going to date. Once when he was gone on one of his tours across the country, I stumbled on his laptop on a boring afternoon. I fiddled with it for an hour but it couldn't keep me engrossed for a long time.

That's when it struck me. I had always believed I was not intelligent enough to be a writer. But I remembered what you had told me. And that you believed I could be a writer. That was when I opened a word document and started typing my mind and eventually carved a story around it. You had planted the thought in my head and that's when it took shape. I started writing my first book and in less than a month it was done. I sent it to all the publishers I could find on the net and went ahead with the one who replied first. The book came out and it struck a chord with the audience. And even though I knew it was a wrong thing to do, I let fame get into my head.

DJ Vyk had been a simple guy with simple needs. He was already a bit famous and I got a bit famous too, together we became a crazy duo. I have no idea when we went from vodka to whisky to cigarettes to weed to hash to Meth. It was a gradual progression and I think I knew what I was getting into. But the gravity which pulled me was way too strong. Sometimes I did it for glamour. Sometimes I did it for harming myself. Sometimes I liked the feeling. Sometimes I just wanted to alter my state of mind, or go into complete blankness. And I am not proud of what I did. But you know right, how and for what reasons people inevitably get into such rebounds,' Navya said.

I was dreading what was coming next. There was something unsure in her eyes. And she said it, 'I missed you, Samar.'

I looked at her, thinking of a suitable response.

'I couldn't live without you,' she continued. 'I needed you in my life. I never thought I could get attached to someone or fall so truly, madly and deeply for anyone. But strangely, without you, the balance in my head was dislodged. And all you wanted was someone else. When I thought I was running away from myself, I was actually running away from you.'

'But nowhere did you realize the magnitude of the puddle you were creating for yourself? You didn't realize how wrong were going? You didn't think of so many people who loved you and who would in pained to see you like that? What *were* you thinking?' I said.

203

'I once wrote a few lines about what I was thinking. Do you want me to read them to you?'

'Yes,' I said.

She brought her phone out of her pocket and started reading.

> *'You know what is the worst thing in the world?*
> *You are amidst this crowd, a swarm of people,*
> *Who think they connect with you,*
> *Every one of them, in their own way.*
> *But in reality, you are being ripped apart,*
> *Connecting with each one of them.*
> *It is a constant struggle to connect with someone,*
> *To be heard, to be understood, to be loved, to be accepted.*
> *And it is done with a glimpse of hope,*
> *That someone from these known and unknown faces,*
> *Will hear you out, someone with a warm & genuine*
> *smile,*
> *Will touch your heart.*
> *And that's precisely when, perhaps, you would say,*
> *'Yes, this is me.'*

* * *

Every Minute Of Your Day

Imran and Joseph helped a great deal in keeping Navya busy. As two days went by without Navya having a dull moment, I finally began to get optimistic about the plan. Definitely, Goa was exuding its healing powers.

On the first day, Navya was immersed in painting. The enthusiasm might not have been as high as it used to be or as we had expected it to be. But she had something to do and keep her mind off drugs. The second day she *came across* a Sophie Kensella book. I bought her latest release because I knew she loved Sophie Kensella and ensured that she found it lying across the hallway.

And things kept happening to her. My confidence began to come back gradually, as I saw her get back on track. I knew the challenge was the two week barrier. If she could go for two weeks without thinking of Meth, she would more or less be through.

I didn't want to let her away from my eyes. But I had another responsibility on my shoulders. There was a dying forty year old who had her hopes on me. I hadn't spoken to her in a week. So I called her number.

She didn't pick my call for a while. And just as it was about to get disconnected, she answered.

'Hi Vandana,' I said. She didn't reply. 'Are you there?' I asked but she didn't speak.

I heard a sharp sound of a woman crying. Vandana was in tears. She was going through the worst kind of torture I could ever imagine. And she disconnected the call.

I was shaken. While I had been in the middle of people I loved, Vandana had probably been banging her head on the walls in an empty flat. She had broken down now. My head froze. My hands got numb. I felt helpless. Leaving her there alone was one of the most regrettable decisions I'd ever taken; I shouldn't have knelt before her powerful convincing powers.

Navya seemed much more stable than she had two weeks back. I needed to get back to get the money together for Vandana. I would have to pass on Navya's responsibility to Joseph for a few days.

'Wow. You *do* know that you are sounding extremely ridiculous, right?' was Joseph's reaction when I told him I had to go and I wanted to leave Navya with him. 'That girl can't go a day without you, Samar. She's at such a sensitive and vulnerable point. What can be so important that you have to leave her at this stage?'

I told him about Vandana and the challenge I had in front of me. Joseph's tone changed after that.

'Hmm. I understand. But by no means can we replace your position, importance and need in Navya's life right now. You need someone closer to her while you are away.'

'What do you mean?'

'I mean like her mother or father or sister or someone. You once took her father's phone number from me. Did you speak to him? Can you call him here?' Navya's father had told me to call him only when Navya was better.

Navya was better. So it was definitely a feasible option. So I went ahead and gave him a call. And told him about the situation and requested him to come to Woodstock as soon as he could.

I was a bit amazed with the speed at which Mr Sharma moved. I called him at four in the afternoon and by eleven on the next morning, he was standing in front of me. He was a well-established builder and I guess it was a part of his business ethics; to show up at various meetings and presentations at short notices.

Mr Sharma couldn't wait to see Navya when I told him that she was much better now and hadn't used Meth in more than a week now.

With a slight tear in his eye, he hugged me and thanked me profusely for the pains I had taken. He again reiterated that being a father, he couldn't have been able to bring his daughter back to life because she was so hostile towards him. He remorsefully regretted that it was his fault that he could not understand his daughter and treat her with more affection and patience.

'So can I take her home now?' he asked, taking charge of his emotions.

'Not at all sir. In fact, she needs to stay here for a few more weeks at least.'

'So what's next then?'

'Actually, I would have to leave Goa for some work. And till then, you would have to take care of her.'

Mr Sharma knew what Navya needed the most at this point was my presence. But he also knew that I wouldn't ask to leave unless it was absolutely important. So he didn't ask me to stay. Instead he asked me what all he had to keep in mind regarding Navya while I was gone.

I introduced Mr Sharma to Joseph and Imran and together we discussed that we would continue with our strategy of keeping her distracted and occupied with the things she loved. And also make sure she doesn't come in contact with any drugs whatsoever. I told them to double check that she has no dull moment which might send her back to unhappy times.

I looked at Mr Sharma in the eye and said, 'You would have to devote every minute of your day to her, without making her realize that you were doing so.'

'It shall be done,' Mr Sharma assured me.

Days You Want To Erase

After executing a happy reunion between Mr Sharma and Navya, I had to re-groove. I had only one number in my head. Fifty lakh rupees. I went to the cyber cafe to check how *www.savevandana.com* was doing. I had expected no miracles; the amount collected was negligible.

I sat in the chair in front of his bed, where he sat. And brought out from my bed the white crystals which had taken me weeks of effort.

'What is this?' Joseph asked, alarmed. I let him take a sample and smell. And the moment he smelt, he knew what it was.

'Get out of this fucking shack Samar! You, of all people, are carrying Meth! Where did you get this shit?'

'Calm down Joseph. Hear me out before you react.'

'There is no story which can justify Meth in your bag Samar. Throw the fuck away this thing,' he said. I couldn't blame him. If I were in his place, I would have reacted in a similar manner.

'Relax, Joseph. There is a life which depends on it. And not just this Meth, but on you too.'

'What do you mean?'

I told him about Vandana, followed by how I had managed to cook Meth in my college lab. If Joseph didn't know me, he might have found it hard to believe. But we had worked together and he held my ability in high regard.

'There must be other options for Vandana which doesn't force people to do what Navya has done to herself,' Joseph said.

'I have explored everything. She doesn't have any family or friends who can help. And fifty lakhs is a big amount,' I said.

'So do you give me your word that you have tried every possible way out and you're sure there is no other option?'

'I give you my word Joseph.'

Joseph looked down and it seemed he remembered God. I was asking him to against his values to save a life. He ran a shack in Goa. Joseph's native town was Kerala but he knew every part of Goa in and out. He must have often been tempted to do things he didn't want for money. He must have had thousands of opportunities. And I was making him give away everything.

'Then tell me what is to be done,' he said.

'I need you to connect me with Meth dealers. And I don't mean people who deal in a few grams. I need someone who deals in dozens of pounds.'

'Okay. I know someone in Goa. But not in Arambol. We would have to go to Margao.'

'What time is the first bus to Margao tomorrow morning?' I asked.

'But there is one condition,' Joseph said.

'What?'

'I help you do this. And you never show me your face again.'

* * *

Joseph's friend's place in Margao had an ancient Portuguese feel to it. This is one of the places the tour guide would take first timers in Goa to, to introduce them to the history of the city. The guy looked more from Haryana than from Mexico, until he opened his mouth. He spoke with Joseph in Konkanese, which suggested he had spent a lot of time in India.

The guy's name was Carlos, possibly the commonest Mexican name. He looked at me top to bottom. Joseph told him what I had and he seemed a little taken aback. I bet I didn't look like a junkie or normal Meth cook.

He gave me a condescending look, declaring that I cannot be good for anything. 'Show me what you have,' he said.

I opened a packet and gave him a bit. He looked at it against the light. And then he smelt it. He carried out every possible analysis he knew. And at the end of it, he seemed convinced with what he saw. I could see on his face that he was impressed.

'Who cooked this?'

'I did.'

'What method did you use?'

'The one with pseudoephedrine.'

'Where did you get the pseudo from?'

'From a pharmacy plant in Manesar. I have a lot of it left with me.'

He asked me a few more technical questions to check how much I knew. I tackled his questions confidently. He was amused by our little adventure. But I had come to understand that where drugs were involved, adventure was a common thing. But it was not a comfortable or healthy adventure.

'So what are you looking for?'

'I know the worth of what I have. The deal is that I cook twenty pounds for you. I will get the raw material. And you will get the equipment. And you give me fifty lakhs.'

'How much time will it take?'

'Depends on your facilities you provide. If you have capacity of four pounds a day, it will be done in five days.'

'Hmm. When can you get started?'

'I need to get started tomorrow itself. I don't have time.'

'Do you have the ingredients with you here?'

'Yes. I had sent them through a transporter to Panjim. He must have got it three days back. I will give you his address. You have you to go and fetch it to your lab. I will get started tomorrow morning.'

'Hmm. I will get that done. Our labs are in Dandeli. It's a two hour drive from here. It is a pretty sheltered space, protected from police or even commoners. We will stay in a room at a lodge nearby.'

In another half an hour, Carlos and I were on the road. Joseph left for Woodstock. As I sat in the car and looked at the barren landscape around us, I opened the calendar on my phone. It was the nineteenth of July.

* * *

You know that feeling when you work hard to achieve something, and then it actually happens and you feel great about it. I mean, imagine making a ten hour journey, spending your one month salary to make a trip to Simla from Delhi. And when you get there, you realize being there doesn't make you any happy? I finally had 5000 notes, worth 1000 rupees each. I was a huge step closer to saving Vandana's life but it didn't make me happy. Perhaps, integrity and peace of mind with happiness can't co-exist. There are days in your life you want to erase from your life. For me, they were those days I spent at the lab in Dandeli.

Anyway, as I sat in the car for the return journey to Goa, I tried closing my eyes and ousting my negative thoughts out. I took a deep breath and told myself that things will only get better from here. My plan was to meet Navya and make sure that she was doing well. And then I would head to Delhi and start Vandana's treatment at the soonest.

I turned on some music on my phone and I was a bit amused by the fact that how long it had been since I had listened to any sort of music. I decided to be less sceptical of give life and give it more chances. It is worth it, I learnt.

On reaching Woodstock, I went straight to Navya's room. Navya was not there, and instead, Mr Sharma was sleeping on the floor in the room. I decided not to disturb him. Instead I went out and started looking for Navya. She was nowhere. So I went inside and woke up Mr Sharma.

When I shook Mr Sharma, I realized he wasn't really sleeping. With a little shake itself, he sat up with a start and looked at me quizzically. And then he looked away, as if he was avoiding eye contact with me.

'Uncle, where is Navya.'

He didn't reply. Instead he went to washroom and I heard a gush of water. I waited outside, hoping that he would take notice of my presence soon. But he didn't. So when he came out, I repeated the question, 'Where is Navya uncle?'

'We couldn't keep her, Samar. She's back to her ways. After you left, she got increasingly restless. And God played a funny joke. There is a group of junkies who came to live at Woodstock. She is out with them. And she's been high ever since they came.'

* * *

I gave up. I had never thought I would say this, especially in reference with Navya, but I gave up on her this time. I believed I had worked too hard on her for her to just betray me like this. And also, there was no doubt in my mind that Vandana needed me more than Navya did now. In fact, as Mr Sharma waited for Navya to show up, I couldn't wait for her to come back. I was disgusted. I had to run out of that place, as soon as I could. So I stopped the same taxi with which I had come, and asked it to take me to the airport.

I bought an air ticket and I took the flight, with thousand rupee notes worth fifty lakhs in my bag. I didn't know it then but it could have been dangerous. If they realize in the scan that there was money worth that much, they could have raised questions. I don't know what saved me. Maybe it was the lousy security check team at the Goa airport. Or maybe it was how harmless I looked. But I landed in Delhi without any hassles.

I headed to Rohini. I hadn't been in touch with Vandana since that phone call.

When I reached home, I saw some clothes let out to dry in the balcony and I knew Vandana was there. The mission was nearing accomplishment. I couldn't wait to see the look on her face when I would open the bag in front of her, and tell her that we *finally* had money for her cure. We would suck the lung cancer out of her body. She would live to see places she hadn't seen till now and do goofy things she didn't know she was capable of.

She was a fighter and I was convinced she would be brave throughout the treatment. The only thing I was worried about was that it was not too late for the treatment to begin. How far would the cancer have progressed in all these months?

All throughout the journey, scary thoughts had clouded my mind. I hoped for the best and prepared for the worst when I rang the doorbell.

My heart began to race, as I rang the bell but no one opened. I rang the bell thrice and when she still didn't reply, I began to panic. I had to decide between trying to bring the door down and calling the duplicate key guy. The most horrific visualizations clouded my head and made it even more difficult for me to decide. I hit the door twice and I realized there was no way I could bring it down. So I ran and fetched the duplicate key guy. And told him how urgent it was. Meanwhile, I called up the ambulance to brace for any spectacle on the other side of the door. If it was a separate lock, I could have broken it down with a brick. But this inbuilt lock was hard to bring down.

I stormed into the house as soon as the door opened. And my heart skipped a beat for a moment. Vandana lay on the floor, lifeless. I ran up to her and checked her pulse.

Pulse was there. Thankfully, the ambulance had arrived by then. They picked her on the stretcher and rushed her inside.

As I looked at her, the same thought came back to my mind.

What could be sadder than waiting for death in a flat, alone?

The Dog In The Fight,
The Fight In The Dog

We reached the Emergency Ward of Rajeev Gandhi Cancer Hospital in Rohini.

Within a couple of minutes, she was entering scanning machines. I waited nervously. The doctor said that they would carry out a list of tests and would only then be able to calculate Vandana's chances of survival.

I didn't have it in me to hear any bad news. Every cell in my body was craving to experience that moment when the doctor would declare that she was going to be alright.

That thought kept me going, counting hours, minutes and seconds till I will get to know. Vandana came out of one machine and entered another. Standing outside, peeping through the glass fence, I could see her unconscious face. I had no idea as to when she would open her eyes. Or if she would ever or not.

When the tests were done, she was moved to a ward. I stared at Vandana unflinching face, I felt if things didn't get back on track soon enough, I would start hallucinating and lose my mental balance. I looked back at the last fifty days. And then I thought of Navya, who was back to square one. And there was Vandana, who looked as dead as anyone can. And then there was me, as far removed from any mental peace as anyone can be.

She had been unconscious for at least ten hours by then but around an hour later, it happened. Her eyelids moved, and then her hand, a little. And I let out a cry of celebration. Her eyes rested on me, and she flashed a faint smile. And then she moved her discoloured lips, collected the wind in her lungs and said, 'You came back.'

'Don't strain your throat,' I told her. And touched her hand to comfort her. She was back, at least for now. The scary ten hours had come to an end. The real test was the meeting I was going to have with the doctor tonight. That's when I would come to know whether she would survive or not.

* * *

When they show important scenes in the movie in slow motion, they're not mistaken. Important incidents do happen in slow motion in real life too. Have you ever been in an accident? Do you remember the last two seconds before the accident when you knew there is going to be an accident and you're about to crash? In hindsight, doesn't the memory of that seem etched in slow and stretched motion? That's how I remember that walk from Vandana's walk to the doctor's room.

The moment I entered, I felt it in the air in the doctor's chamber. I saw the expression on his face, I knew I didn't have to wait for words to make my worst fears come true.

'For how long have you known about the cancer?' the doctor asked.

'For around four months.'

'She badly needed the surgery then itself. Why was it delayed?'

'The surgery was expensive,' I replied.

The doctor looked back into one of the reports in his hand. He gathered his thoughts before he spoke and said, 'Vandana has lung cancer, which is a curable cancer if detected early. In this case, even though the cancer was detected early, it wasn't treated at that time. And now, the cancer has spread all over her chest.'

The doctor pulled out an X-ray report and showed it to me.

'Can you see this thick white cloud all over her chest? This is all cancer. Look how extensively it has spread.'

I was worried that any moment now, the doctor was going to say that it was incurable now.

'What should we do now?' I asked.

'We need to carry out her surgery within this week. That's the first step. It's a complex surgery. And I would have to invite doctors from outside. It's going to be expensive.'

'And what are her chances, doctor?'

'Listen, Samar. I appreciate your courage in handling so much responsibility at this age. But this is a complex surgery. It will cost almost 30-40 lakhs. I'm not going to give you false hopes; even if the body takes the surgery well, the chances of her survival are almost negligible. I know you are not her blood relative, but in such cases the most loving families opt for not going for the surgery. I don't know whether you can arrange that sort of money or not. What I'm saying is that there is a very little chance that money would be able to save her.'

I was close to tears. The doctor was telling me that

it was too late already. I had failed to put the money together in time. Vandana was going to die, definitely. I didn't know what to say. I got up from my seat, without really ending the meeting. I began to exit, not knowing what to say, think or do.

And just as I was about to exit, I looked at the doctor and said to him, 'Start preparing for the surgery, sir'.

* * *

On the day of the surgery, I was with Vandana, holding her hand, comforting her that it was all going to be okay. The doctor told me that I could stay there till they gave her anaesthesia.

I had deposited thirty lakhs in the hospital account and the doctors had been working hard for a few days to prepare for the surgery. I checked the date, it was the fifth of August. My college had started and I couldn't have felt more disconnected from college than I was feeling then.

The last week had been a painful one for Vandana. She was eating more medicines than food every day. Her lip and her smile had dried up and she was losing strength at a very fast pace. When I told her about Navya's relapse into drugs, she got really sad. But she didn't cry, probably because her tears had dried up by now.

'And you left Navya to come to Delhi?' she said, accusingly.

'My job in Delhi was equally important, if not more.'

'Where did you get the money, Samar?' she enquired.

She believed me when I told her that *savevandana.com* had finally taken off and people from all over the world had donated for her treatment.

'Internet is such a wonderful thing,' she said.

As the anaesthesia was injected into her body she began to lose consciousness. As her eyes closed, she mumbled a name. And I knew what was the next thing I needed to do. It was a twelve hour surgery. I realized that as Vandana was unconscious, I didn't need to be there. So I decided to get busy with preparing the biggest surprise she could ever get on gaining consciousness.

* * *

At around two in the night, she opened her eyes. I was looking through the glass window. There were only two people in the room. One was Vandana, the other was her, smiling away, holding her hand.

It was Divya, whose name Vandana had taken before lapsing into unconsciousness. After a brief silence, the ward came alive at two in the night with the sound of two women hugging, weeping, smiling and talking. It was a sight that I extract from my memory and visit sometimes. It gives me strength. It defines silver lining for me.

Meanwhile, the doctor patted on my back. We both knew it. Even before the operation. But he made me come to terms with it with that senile smile.

'How much time does she have doctor?'

'Possibly a month or so.'

Both the doctor and I witnessed through the glass, the cathartic cry of Vandana. Life *had* come a full circle for her. She found her true love after all these years. Divya looked aged and matured, as she held Vandana. She had cried her share when I went to her place to inform her about Vandana's position. She confessed that she could never find true love after Vandana left her. She realized that a person realizes another person's worth only in their absence. But this was it. At least one of us had attained inner peace, even though it was just for one final month. The part of her which had been missing was now found. She was now complete.

The Wind Beneath My Wings

It's hard to leave people behind. I had been talking to Mr Sharma every day. He was spending every day in Goa, watching his daughter doing everything she shouldn't. Every passing day was weighing heavily on him. And leaving Vandana into Divya's hands, I could now concentrate back on Navya.

When I talked to him last, I listened to him intently. He told me how he was trying to cure her in Goa. He told me what he thought we should do next. He was worried and he was desperate. He had stranded his business and everything else just to get his daughter back. WoodStock Village was not the right place any more. It was as if the place had been polluted by Meth now. If it was not for Navya, Joseph would have thrown each of those junkies out in no time.

There was only one other place where I could take her. The Ashram. Perhaps, Swamiji was the therapist she needed. It was a long shot, but I had great faith in Swamiji's abilities.

I sat in the bus to Rishikesh, which was where I was going to meet Navya. I had to scold her to make her come to Rishikesh. It was the seventh of August now.

All my hopes of getting placed in a good company on campus were blown away. If I was talking to my mom, she would have lost her cool on this. But she had been sweet enough to let me be by myself. I knew it must be tearing her apart but she was patient and letting me do what I wanted to do. This was the strength of her love.

I reached Rishikesh and met Navya at the bus stand itself. She was back to looking terrible, like a typical addict. And she was back to having a blank look in her eyes. I had every reason to give up. In fact, I knew I didn't have it in me to mend something so broken. The only thing which kept me going was that it was not me who was going to be responsible this time. It would be Swamiji. And I had great faith in his ability to change people.

* * *

When Navya and I went and sat in front of Swamiji, he didn't speak for a while. He kept studying her face for what seemed to me like five minutes.

'Welcome to The Ashram, Navya,' Swamiji said.

'Thank you Swamiji. It's great to be here.'

'But there is a catch in your stay here. Your soul is polluted by the drugs. You would have to leave that part of your soul outside The Ashram when you enter here.'

'Detach a part of soul? What do you mean?'

'Don't worry. I don't mean to scare you. I just want you to do one simple thing for me. Close your eyes and tell yourself that you are not a drug addict. You will not do this ever again, not because you don't *have* to, but because you don't *want* to. You will tell yourself that you have no urge to do it again. You will tell yourself that it was a dark chapter of your life, which is now over. And you will mean it when you will say it to yourself. Once and for all, take a journey through whatever you've been through and command your soul to retain the pleasant ones. Think of drugs as a ferocious predator, eating away your positive thoughts. Respect your life, Navya. Plant faith in your potential of art and creativity. Being a servant to a chemically altered mind is not cool. It is a sign of weakness. Close your eyes and bring your strength back. I know you have a lot of will power, get so much of it that you can help others out in the endeavour to reach Inner Peace.'

Navya was a bit baffled for a second. But Swamiji had such an aura that she obliged, and closed her eyes. Swamiji and I looked on, as her expressions started getting strained. It seemed as if she was remembering some bad memories, possibly of her father. And then she smiled, as her thoughts were replaced by something more pleasant. I had a feeling she was thinking of our time in Goa, the first time around. I don't know about her but Swamiji's stupefying words resounded in my ears.

'Respect your life. Plant faith in your potential of art and creativity. You're not a servant to a chemically altered mind. It is a sign of weakness.'

As her expressions then turned sad again and then got flat, Swamiji and I waited in anticipation of what is going to happen next.

I believe it was a good ten to fifteen minutes later when she got a broad smile on her face. I hadn't seen her smiling that heartily for a long time. And I knew she was up to something special. And then, she opened her eyes

225

slowly, and the smile only got broader. And she stared at Swamiji, as if the last fifteen minutes were nothing short of a rebirth for her. I was ecstatic on seeing her like that. Swamiji had done his magic. Without doing anything, he had changed her frame of mind completely.

'How does it feel Navya?' he asked.

'Better,' Navya said after thinking for a second. She wasn't a girl of many words, but when she said better, it meant things were only going to get better from here.

'I want to tell you something Navya. And you too Samar. We are nothing but the mistakes we make. And everybody makes mistakes. That's what makes us human. It's important to forgive yourself for those mistakes and accept yourself with them instead of ruing yourself over it forever. We have a tendency to relapse into the mistakes we've made once, because we feel we have been there once, we could do it again. But that is where your inner strength, friends, family, passions, books, and love will play a role. Distract yourself to positivity and let life surprise you with its rewards.'

Navya nodded her head.

Swamiji continued, 'And *beta*, no irreversible damage has been done. All you have to do is detox yourself in a certain way and I will help you do that. And then, you would go back to your life, finish your studies and become a wonderful person you were always going to be.'

'*Ji* Swamiji. I assure you I will try my best,' Navya said. Within a few minutes of meeting Swamiji, she was beginning to talk positively, which we hadn't been able to achieve in months. By then, I had completely confident that Swamiji is going to take full care of her. She was in good hands and finally, after months of running around, I could breathe in peace.

'Tell me one thing Navya, what is love according to you,' Swamiji said.

'Well Swamiji, in my opinion, love is trust. The belief that someone will not leave me for the world, will be there beside me in good and bad times, and will love me, when I would have nothing to offer him, is what I believe love is.'

Swamiji nodded with a faint smile. And then he looked at me. 'The same question to you, Samar. What do you think love is?'

I had to think a little bit. Unlike Navya, I had never really sat and thought what is love.

'According to me, love is happiness. If she makes me feel happy with her presence and her absence sucks the happiness out of me, I love her.'

Swamiji nodded again in his characteristic style.

'So Navya, do you trust Samar? Do you believe he will not leave you for the world? Do you think he will there beside you in good and bad times? And that he will love you, when you would have nothing to offer him?'

Navya smiled. And then she looked down. I had known her for over a year and this coyness was a completely new expression on her. It was the biggest confirmation she could have given.

Without a verbal reply from Navya, Swamiji turned to me. 'Tell me Samar,' he said, 'does Navya make you feel happy with her presence? Does her absence suck the happiness out of you?'

227

Swamiji had made his point. And his point was that Navya and I were in love without realizing so. Or maybe, we did realize it but had never said it out aloud, even to ourselves. But he wanted to break that barrier. Sometimes it's important to state the obvious too.

'Now I want you two to answer a question for me. Samar and Navya, are you in love with each other?'

Swamiji was playing the perfect cupid. He is not the kind of person you would expect to be playing a matchmaker. But he had a very valid reason. It was as if as he was staring at Navya, he was making up his mind that whether we were the perfect match or not.

There was a pin drop silence in the room when he asked that. The topic had been under the carpet for a while.

'Yes, I am in love with her,' I spoke first. It had to be said. There was no doubt in my head and Navya deserved to hear it. And I wanted to say it before she did. Navya looked at me. She got up from her cross legged posture. I stood up too.

'I love you too Samar,' she said softly. And there, in front of Swamiji, in an Ashram in Rishikesh, in a *kutiya* made of thatch, I felt heaven.

Navya was in my arms, her head on my shoulder, her breath on my collar bone, my arm around her back, her hair touching my cheek, culmination of months of anticipation, the moment we had waited for and it had taken Swamiji to push us over the edge, into an unending abyss of happiness.

We left the *kutiya* for the day. As I walked out of the *kutiya*, I realized I was holding her hand. We walked silently, not knowing what to talk about. But still, there

228

was infinite joy in our hearts, there was nothing awkward about the silent walk.

We went Navya's room and closed the door behind us. And our lips met, with more passion than I thought was possible. There was no awkwardness of having Swamiji looking at us this time. And with smooth, and gentle movements, I removed her clothes one after the other, as she removed mine. And we made chaotic, unrehearsed, messy but very passionate love that night.

And that was the moment things turned around for Navya. She attained her share of inner peace at that moment. She transformed from a disturbed drug addict to a love struck regular twenty year old in that moment. The Ashram had done its magic. And the old, broken Navya was now left behind, forever.

* * *

The second day with Swamiji was a bit different. Navya and I entered the *kutiya* holding each other's hands.

I had a feeling what was going to happen today. The last time I had been under Swamiji's haven, he had told me three things. The first thing he had told me was that it's okay to be wrong. He had already talked about it yesterday. The second thing he had told me was that I need to help everyone I can help. I had a feeling he was going to talk about that today.

As he welcomed us and asked us how we were doing, I waited for him to throw the awkward question at me.

'So who all did you help Samar, since I told you to help people?'

I was a bit ashamed. I had seriously not helped anyone

and hence just hung my head in shame. Honestly, I hadn't taken Swamiji's teachings that seriously.

'Samar, look at me,' he said. 'Why are you so harsh on yourself? Since you left The Ashram, you were trying to help both Navya and Vandana, without any selfish motives. You spoilt your summer internship and are now missing your placement season and have no regret about missing them. I respect you for that.'

'Thank you Swamiji,' I said, with lifted spirits.

'But you need to do more work. You have to help a few more people before you attain peace in yourself,' Swamiji said, looking at Navya.

'Who are you talking about?'

'Navya, who took care of you after you came to Delhi?'

'DJ Vyk,' she said. And everything became clear to her. DJ Vyk was himself a drug addict. Navya had abandoned him and come with Samar. It was time she met him again. And brought about his resurrection

Navya took the next bus to Delhi, the same night. I went to the station to say bye to her. I wasn't comfortable with letting her out of my sight but then one has to make tough decisions sometimes.

I came back to The Ashram after dropping her. It was an important night for me. This was the night when a lot of my doubts would get solved.

Vandana was now with Divya, waiting for her end, but in the arms of the person she loved the most, having definitely attained her inner peace. She must be sleeping better at nights when she had no pain.

And Navya was definitely at peace with herself now.

She had the love of her life and was now on a mission to make DJ Vyk get rid of drugs.

The big question now was that whether I had attained inner peace or not. And this was the night which would tell me. I first went to the evening *arti* and went and sat in a corner. I hadn't been alone in a while and having come so far, my heart was still not at rest.

The holy chant of *'Hare Rama, Hare Krishna'*, was going on nonstop in front of me. I looked at faces around me, people were being touched deep inside by that chant. It was as if the chant was doing things to them that drugs did to people. They were absorbing it, they were under its beautiful spell.

But as I sat there, listening to the same chant as other people, I felt I was blind to what they were feeling. I was happy because I was in love, but still something was bothering me deep inside. I had one more day left with Swamiji. And I had tons of questions for him. Perhaps, he had a trick or two up his sleeves for me too.

* * *

The next evening, I was sitting in front of Swamiji, alone for the first time. There was neither Vandana, nor Navya next to me for the first time. It was just me and him. And I knew I was the only one left.

As I sat there, with a wrinkle on my forehead, I had no doubt in my mind that Swamiji would know in a second what was going through my head.

'How are you feeling Samar?' he asked. I had a feeling he knew what I was going to say.

'I'm still not feeling the way I normally should, Swamiji.

Everything is done now. Vandana is in peace and Navya is in peace. This is what I wanted all this while. And now that it has happened, I am still not at peace with myself. And I have no idea why. I can't put my finger on what is bothering me. But I know that I am not okay. I still can't sleep well. I still can't be stable. And you are my only hope, Swamiji. If you don't have answers to my questions, I'll be broken. '

Swamiji dropped his smile for the first time since I had been seeing him. He seemed serious for the first time. It sounded like bad news for me.

'Samar, you remember the last thing I told you? That you need to stop trying to be somebody else and embrace who you are. That is your problem. That's what you need to do,' he said. 'And I am sure you still don't have any idea of what I am talking about.'

I shook my head.

'What is the saddest incident of your life?' Swamiji asked. And I knew where he was headed at that moment itself.

'Kanika's death,' I said, without any hesitation.

'And when was the last time you talked to anyone about it?'

I thought about it.

A few lines that Navya had once said were coming to my mind. Nothing else described my feelings at that time better than them.

> *'You know what's the worst thing in the world?*
> *You are amidst this crowd, swarm of people,*

who think they connect with you,
every one of them, in their own way.
But in reality, you are being ripped apart,
Connecting with each one of them.
It is a constant struggle to connect with someone,
To be heard, to be understood, to be loved, to be accepted.
And it is done with a glimpse of hope,
That someone from these known and unknown faces,
Will hear you out, someone with a warm & genuine smile,
Will touch your heart.

And that's precisely when, perhaps, you would say,
'Yes, this is me.'

Swamiji was taken aback by my rant. I must have sounded like I was recalling these lines instead of blabbering whatever was coming to my mind.

'You can't run away from it for the rest of your life. You need to stop trying to be a guy who has had no set back and is completely normal. The truth is that you had a sad incident in your life and you need to accept that.'

'I think I have handled it and that I am in love again, which is true, but I still can't forget Kanika's death.'

'Lie down Samar. Get comfortable and close your eyes. I want you to be completely relaxed and surrender your thoughts to me. Your problems are very deeply ingrained in your head and I would have to delve deep inside to root them out.'

I stretched my arms and lied down in front of him. And waited for him to speak.

'Why do you not let yourself think of Kanika, Samar? Why do shove her thoughts away? Did you fall in love with her on the condition that she will love you back? Or is it that you think you won't be able to love another soul until you don't stop thinking of her?'

'I don't know. All I know is . . . thinking of her makes me extremely, extremely uneasy and restless. It's painful, very painful for me.'

'But you would have to man up to this and embrace your past like you've embraced your present. You will have to accept what happened.'

'It's more complex than that. You were not there.'

'I know what is complex, Samar. I wasn't there but I know what happened. Do you know what is the biggest question in your head?'

'What?'

'That whether you were responsible for what happened or not. And the answer is obviously you were responsible. You were a weak lover if you believed that Kanika could kiss another guy. You were stubborn when she came all the way to meet you to Goa and you would just not give her chance to speak to you. You were coward when you ran away from her and you keep running away from things. That is not how life works Samar. You can't keep messing up and keep running away from your mess. You need to accept the person you have been and live it through. Sure you can amend things that you don't like about yourself now but gracefully accept the weaknesses of your past.'

My eyes were closed as I lay down on the floor. I was hearing every word coming out of his mouth, as images of my time with Kanika flashed in front of my eyes.

Happy memories. Sad memories. It all came by. But I let my thoughts flow. I let every thought come to me which I had blocked out for so long now.

And with a heart heavier than it had ever been before, I let out the most gut wrenching cry that ever escaped my body.

Epilogue

The last Vandana spoke with her parents was years ago, when she attempted to call them up and tell them about her cancer.

'Hello? *Papaji*?' said a quivering Vandana.

'Vandana? So you do remember that you have parents?' he said, with an expected stern tone.

'I'm sorry, Papa. How's *mummyji*?

'Leave her. Tell us about the boy because of whom you forgot us. Are you calling to tell us about how that *khotta* went away leaving you with two kids?' asked Mr Manchanda, smugly and without a tinge of pity in this voice.

'I haven't married yet, Papa. And that is because I fell in love with a girl. With Divya,' said Vandana, combating her father's tone confidently now.

He stayed quiet for twenty seconds and then said, *'Humaare marne pe bhi apni shakal mat dikhaana.' (Don't dare to show up even on my death).* And with that, he hung up.

Vandana recollected this scene in the hospital, on her deathbed.

'Of course there is a sharp increase in the unbearable heaviness of

237

being,' she said and laughed, thinking she cracked a funny joke, but, then, sobering, she said, 'there is also a want to give up.'

She tried cracking another joke to lighten the strain in the room, 'So there is another advantage with painful deaths, it'll definitely be better the moment you leave the painful diseased body.'

She knew it a couple of days before her death that she was going to die. She said, laughingly, that she had seen it in movies that a person comes to know when they are dying. Like a few species of animals come to know beforehand about an earthquake. And two days' later, she ratified it for us. She died.

It was difficult for Divya. She had re-discovered her true love after years. She was forever indebted to Vandana for showing her that kind of love.

Both her and Kanika's death were not a painful memory for me now. I had learnt to accept past and appreciate life. It was beautiful while it lasted and I helped Divya understand this too.

Navya went through her eight weeks of therapy and rehab along with DJ Vyk and both of them came out clean. Post that, Navya went to Indore to meet her family. Things were bound to bridge between her and her father. And then, finally, she came to Delhi, to live with me. She started writing her second book. Every second of her smiling face was like a gift to me.

As for me, the day that I came out of the Ashram, I made the most important phone call of that period of my life. I called Mom. And everything felt complete.

● ● ●

COMING SOON

from

SACHIN GARG

WE NEED A

REVOLUTION

Other Book by the same author

Before Come On, Inner Peace happened, Samar and Kanika were a happy couple, which made every one jealous.

Read about their love in the prequel to this book - **Never Let Me Go.**

Order your copy online or in a bookstore near you.